Journey to the Vol

Rose Tremain is a novelisks
include *Sadler's Birthday*, *a*,
The Colonel's Daughter and s a
featured author in the Book Marketing Council's promotion The
Best of Young British Novelists and in 1984 won the Dylan
Thomas Short Story Award. *Journey to the Volcano* is her first book
for young readers.

Rose Tremain lives with her husband and daughter in Norwich.

Rose Tremain

JOURNEY
TO THE
VOLCANO

illustrated by
Alan Marks

PAN PIPER
PAN MACMILLAN
CHILDREN'S BOOKS

First published 1985 by Hamish Hamilton Ltd
This Piper edition published 1988 by Pan Books Ltd,
Cavaye Place, London SW10 9PG
6 8 9 7
© Rose Tremain 1985
All rights reserved
ISBN 0 330 29360 5
Phototypeset by Parker Typesetting Service, Leicester
Printed and bound in Great Britain by
Cox & Wyman Ltd, Reading, Berkshire

CONTENTS

For Eleanor, Kate and Edmund,
with love and lipsicles
where the lizards run

1

Moses Friday

That day, George Lewis decided not to go to school.

It was ten to nine and sunny in the park. George felt peculiar. He felt wicked, dreamy, light in his head. He'd never missed school till then. He thought of his friends going in: Steve Gish, Mat Beamish, Eddie Fenbow. He thought of his empty place and Miss Dowding calling out his name, George Lewis.

George Lewis is in the park. George Lewis is feeling strange. No one in the world knows where George Lewis is.

He wanted to do something exciting. He wished he was by the sea. He wished he was by the sea on a galloping horse.

People were scuttling across the park and he sat on a bench and looked at them: men in suits, women with clacking heels, all off to offices, using the park as a short cut. Life is boring, thought George. It's the boredom of life making me feel weird.

He heard a clock strike nine. The office people hurried away. An old woman passed him, keeping obediently to the path, and she smiled. She wore a black coat. The black coat on the old woman reminded George of his grandmother,

Violetta. And it was then that he knew where he wanted to be that day: he wanted to be on Violetta's mountain! On that mountain, life wasn't boring. On that mountain, there were lemon trees and wine for all the children at suppertime and fat, near-seeming stars. And, best of all, saddest of all, there was his mother, Anna . . .

'Anna, Anna . . .' George whispered to the empty park, 'Anna, Mamma . . .'

Miss Dowding calls out George's name in the classroom, but he doesn't hear it.

George calls out Anna's name in the park, but she doesn't hear it.

Life is peculiar.

George sighed and opened his lunch box and at five past nine ate a tuna sandwich and a Bounty bar.

But then, he decided after all – because the park was boring, because no amount of wishing could actually take him to Violetta's mountain – to go to school. When he arrived there, he told Miss Dowding that he was late because he'd been at the vet's with his dog, Garibaldi.

'Oh,' said Miss Dowding. 'What's the matter with your dog?'

George looked down at his feet. 'His feet hurt,' he said.

'I'm sorry,' said Miss Dowding kindly.

At George's elbow, Eddie Fenbow giggled. The class was doing R.E. They were drawing pictures of the baby Moses in his basket among the bullrushes. Steve Gish had drawn a speech bubble coming out of his baby-basket and had written 'I am Ed Moses' in gold outliner. George sat next to Steve Gish (known as 'Gishy'). Gishy was his best friend.

'I've been in the park,' George whispered, starting his picture of Moses.

'What for?' asked Gishy, colouring stars and stripes on his baby-basket.

'I just felt like it. I ate my lunch.'

'Why? Can't your dad afford breakfast?'

'Yeh.'

'Why, then?'

'I don't get bored when I'm eating.'

'You're weird, Lewis.'

'I'm not.'

'Please be quiet!' said Miss Dowding, lifting her head from her marking.

'It's your Italian blood,' whispered Gishy.

'Sicilian blood,' corrected George.

George Lewis was eleven. His hair was thick and dark. His father, Robert, was English, but his mother, Anna, was Sicilian and had spent her childhood in Aquilone, Violetta's village on the low slopes of Mount Etna. From the age of fifteen, Anna had worked in a china shop in Taormina, a little town very popular with the tourists, and it was here, going in to buy a pair of candlesticks, that Robert had met her and fallen in love with her. Three months later, they had been married. A year later, George was born. The pair of candlesticks stood on the mantelpiece of their London house, and whenever Robert looked at them, he thought of the happiness they had brought him.

Anna and Robert had taken George to Aquilone when he was a baby the size of Moses in the bullrushes. His Uncle

Enzo had given Anna silver coins to bring luck and strength to her son. There had been songs sung for him and wine drunk for him. There was eating and dancing and clapping and the shining of the fat stars.

Since then, he'd been to Aquilone three times. There was a cousin, Guido, one year older than George, but shorter, with wide, fleshy hands and curly hair. There were smaller children who, in summer, went barefoot in the stone houses. Last year, there had been a new baby, Filomena, the largest, hungriest child to come out of Aunt Sofia's big comfy womb. Guido and George had taken the baby for walks in her old, heavy pram, while Aunt Sofia and Anna cooked supper and Robert sat with Enzo and his friends on hard chairs, drinking wine at sundown. Guido and George showed little Filomena the olive trees that were Enzo's pride and joy and the almond trees that bloomed before the winter had properly gone, and the tall cypresses, planted by Filomena's ancestors at the gates of the Aquilone cemetery where her grandfather, Vincente, was buried. One day, Guido dug up a worm and dangled it in front of the baby's face. Filomena gurgled at the worm. *'Il verme! Il verme!'* Guido instructed. And when she started to cry, he whistled a song to her. 'Very rude song,' he told George, 'so I don't tell her the words!'

George laughed, but he felt outdone by Guido. He wanted to teach things to Filomena, so he sang her *Old Ab'ram Brown is Dead and Gone*.

'What is "dedagone"?' asked Guido.

'Dead and *gone*,' repeated George. 'It means "finished", "kaput", "*finito*", "*la morte*".'

Whenever George remembered an Italian word, he felt pleased. He was slightly ashamed of his father for not being able to speak Anna's language.

Guido had friends in the village. One was a big, angry-looking boy called Fabio. Fabio told the most fantastic lies. He said there were leopards on the mountain, he said there were forty-seven earth tremors on the day he was born. George was a bit uneasy with Fabio. Sometimes he would leave the two older boys and come and find Anna, who spent most of her days talking to Grandmother Violetta. George had never heard his mother talk as much as she did with Violetta.

Violetta's house, some way above the village itself, was small, but cool and tidy, with a little stone terrace where the women sat and shelled beans and talked. Very often, they talked about Nonno Vincente, Grandfather Vincente, who had died of pneumonia in the freezing winter of 1972, two years before George was born. Talking about Vincente didn't seem to make them sad. In fact, it seemed to George that, with her memories of her father and with her baskets and colanders of beans, his mother was very happy.

And when they'd left Aquilone, on the last visit, Anna had cried. She had cried all the way home in the plane. Robert had bought her a little bottle of wine to cheer her up, but she said she didn't want the wine or the meal the air stewardess offered her. So Robert just turned away from Anna crossly and read his newspaper and Anna continued to cry. It seemed to George that this happened quite often now: his father going silent, getting cross behind his newspaper; his mother weeping for her Sicilian family, for the lost moments of the bean shelling. And this state of affairs made George afraid. He'd begun to suspect that something bad was going to happen, but when the bad thing came, it was much worse than he'd imagined.

Anna had one friend where they lived in south London. She was called Serafima Smith. She was Sicilian like Anna and married to an Englishman called Sefton Smith. Her family lived in Messina, on the north-east tip of the island of Sicily.

One Tuesday morning, while Robert Lewis sat in his office in the Oceana Life Assurance Building, Anna Lewis had packed a small suitcase and moved out of the house where she'd lived with her husband for twelve years. She went to stay with Serafima Smith, whose spare room was blue and calm. She left a note for George. The note said simply: *Please forgive your mother for going away. Your father will explain.*

But Robert hadn't explained. He'd gone into his own room to read Anna's letter to him and closed the door. George had waited. He had guessed that the leaving had something to do with Sicily, but he didn't really know what. Robert had come out of his room and given George £2 to buy fish and chips for their supper. There had been a queue at the chippy. George had wondered whether, when he got home, his father would have disappeared too. He ran back. His father was in his usual chair, reading the newspaper. Eating the thick salty chips, George had said: 'She's coming back, isn't she?' Robert had looked away. Robert Lewis was a thin man with narrow grey eyes and neat brown hair that was fading. 'The note doesn't say,' said Robert.

'She wouldn't just leave us and not come back,' said George. 'Would she?'

'She's unhappy,' said Robert.

'Why's she unhappy, Dad?'

'It's hard to say.'

'Because she misses Sicily and Nonna Violetta?'

'Maybe. Now eat up, George. It's no use us moping.'

So. They didn't want him to know. He was eleven. At twelve, Guido seemed to know everything about Aunt Sofia and Uncle Enzo. Perhaps, in England, people tried harder to keep everything secret?

When George told Gishy his mother had left them, Gishy said: 'Well, if she's a Catholic, it's probably something to do with the Pope.' Eddie Fenbow said: 'I doubt it. The Pope's not interested in women.' Mat Beamish said: 'It's probably definitely to do with sex.' Gishy said Eddie and Mat were wallies and took George on one side and said, 'Don't listen to those creeps. They're growing up to be idiots.'

George didn't cry. He certainly didn't want anyone to feel sorry for him. But he felt peculiar. Sort of rearranged in his head. He wondered if he was in a state of shock.

The behaviour of his father was extraordinary because it was so ordinary. He watched his usual TV programmes, he made omelettes for their suppers or heated frozen dinners, not seeming to miss the rich stews and pasta dishes Anna used to make. The house was quiet without Anna, and in this quietness Robert Lewis made simple arrangements for the everyday kinds of things: the tidying of rooms, the cooking, the changing of laundry. Life just goes on, he seemed to be saying. You go to work at the Oceana Life

Assurance Company, you come home, you read the paper, you cook, you wash up, you take Garibaldi for a walk on Clapham Common, you listen to the news, you go to bed. You're not exactly sad, just quiet. You don't speak of what used to be. You don't even think about it.

In this quiet, unchanging way, six weeks had passed. Anna didn't come to visit them, nor did she telephone. George wanted to go round to Serafima's house. It was only a busride away. But he didn't go. He'd decided that Anna was probably recovering from something and would like to be left alone. He imagined her lying in bed till late, snoozing in the warm afternoons. He was afraid to disturb her.

Then came the Friday, the day when George said Anna's name out loud in the park, the day when the class drew baby Moses. It was June. There were bees on the flowering shrubs outside the headmaster's window. There was a month of term left.

George had invited Gishy to tea. Robert had said he'd leave the boys money for swimming. When school ended that afternoon, they left Eddie and Mat and the rest of their class and started to walk together towards the bike sheds. Suddenly, Gishy stopped and tugged George's arm.

'Hey!' he said. 'There's your mother.'

George looked towards the school gates. There stood Anna. Kids, streaming out of school, rode or walked by her. She looked anxiously at them all, searching for George. As soon as he saw her, George dropped his school bag and ran to her. 'Oh!' said Anna, as he buffeted into her. 'I *miss* you, Giorgio! I miss you!'

Now, George felt like crying. Now, being with her again, he knew how terrible it was that she'd gone away. 'Please come home,' he said.

But quickly, still holding him closely to her, Anna started to walk away from the school, turning left instead of right at the gate.

'Listen to me, Giorgio,' she began to say, 'we're going to have a secret adventure.'

George looked up at her and he saw that her face was serious and set. Excitement and fear rolled through him. He heard Gishy call to him, but he didn't turn his head. Something was coming. He'd felt it that morning in the park. Something wicked and wonderful. He was ready for it.

'Where are we going, Mamma?' he asked.

Anna clapped her hand over his mouth. 'Ssh!' she said. 'You don't ask me yet. I tell you, this is secret.'

At the corner of the street, Serafima Smith was waiting in her car. 'Get in quickly,' instructed Anna. And hardly had George closed his door before the car sped off down the road. George looked back for a second at the school and saw Gishy standing, staring, in the middle of the road.

2

Lies and Accidents

Gishy took George's bike and his school bag home with him and covered them with old sacks in his father's garden shed.

He'd watched George drive off with Anna and Serafima and had memorised the car number, OBJ 552W, till he could write it on his hand. This, and the hiding of George's bike, made Gishy feel he was a kind of detective. There had been something odd about the way George's mother had bundled him into the car, a bit like a kidnapper. And only he, Gishy, knew who had taken him.

Gishy suspected that, later on, Robert Lewis would telephone, or even turn up, asking about George. What should Gishy do then? What would George want him to do? Should he tell Robert what he'd seen, or not? He couldn't decide. He stared at the hidden bike. Should he tell what he knew or tell a lie? Gishy quite liked the feeling of power this choice gave him. I'll decide which to do later on, he thought.

When, later on, Gishy's mother came in, she said, 'I thought you were going to have tea with George and Steven.'

'I was,' said Gishy, 'but he was sick in Assembly. He had to go home.'

'Oh,' said his mother, 'I see.'

Gishy turned away from her, blushing. He'd told his first lie. Lies would probably be easy from now on.

Robert Lewis usually got home at six. The Oceana Life Assurance Company was an Australian firm and, during these weeks while Anna was away, Robert was working hard on a new savings offer to his clients called the Boomerang Bonus Plan. Robert thought that the word 'boomerang' was neat for the plan. The idea was, you saved and saved, and one day your money boomeranged right back to you. Robert knew that his job wasn't a terribly interesting one, but he was, after the invention of the Boomerang Bonus Plan, quite proud of his company.

Robert Lewis was thirty-five. He was the kind of man who never told people much about himself because he didn't think they'd be interested. He was always polite and nice, but he seemed rather fond of sitting in silence. His favourite things were going to the opera and watching the news on TV. He was a good father – a bit dull sometimes – and he was very loyal. He liked life to run smoothly and quietly, but before she'd left him, Anna had made it all noisy, crying for her mother, Violetta, and for Sicily and sometimes accusing Robert of not loving her.

Actually, Robert loved Anna very much, but he found ctionate things terribly difficult to say. He wished he d have sung them, like at the opera: *Oh, when I am my adored one, remember how much I loved you!* He was depressed now and then. His own littleness in a gigantic world depressed him. He would have liked to be larger and more important – a famous opera singer, for instance. He sometimes cheered himself up by joining things. Last year, he'd joined the SDP.

He got home that Friday at his usual time. On weekdays, it was George who took Garibaldi out at four and Robert who walked him again later. The first thing Robert heard that day as he came down the short path to his door was Garibaldi whining and scrabbling at the front door. Robert opened the door. Garibaldi rushed past him into the garden. Robert thought, oh those silly boys, they forgot to let the dog out. But then he saw the money he'd left them for the swimming pool still on the table. He called out, but he knew it was a waste of time. There was no sign of George's bike. No one had been home.

He went into the kitchen. 'Where is he? Where is he?' he said aloud. His heart was beating very fast. He put the kettle on. Keep calm, he told himself. He must be at Steve Gish's house.

Gishy was having tea when the telephone rang. With his mouth full of sausage, he got up to answer it, but his mother put her hand out, pushing him back into his chair.

'You can't go to the telephone with your mouth full, Steven,' she said. 'Just sit down.'

'But I know it's for me,' Gishy said.

'Finish your mouthful,' said his mother. 'Just do as I tell you!'

Gishy knew – every nerve in his body knew – that it was Robert Lewis on the telephone. The time was 6.10. He would have come home from his office and found the house empty and the swimming money still on the table . . .

'Hello,' said Mrs Gish, snatching up the receiver.

There was a long silence. Gishy struggled to swallow his sausage and waited. His mother was looking straight at him when he heard her say: 'I'm sorry, Mr Lewis, I'm afraid he isn't. I understand from Steven that he was ill this morning and went home after Assembly.'

There was another long silence. Gishy's mother was a rather beautiful woman, of whom he was often a bit afraid. He was afraid of her now as she said sharply:

'Steven, it's George Lewis's father. What did you tell me happened to George today?'

Gishy coughed. Lies squeezed your lungs. They choked you.

'He was sick in Assembly,' said Gish faintly.

'Are you sure he went home?'

'Yeah.'

'Who accompanied him home?'

'Accompanied him?'

'Yes. Don't look so idiotic. Who accompanied him home?'

'Dunno.'

'You must know. Don't be so stupid. You're in his class.'

'Dunno. The nurse, I expect.'

He was choking. He went to the sink and ran some water into a glass. His mother kept watching him as she said: 'Steven thinks it was the school nurse who went home with him.'

Again, there was a silence. Gishy went back to his tea, but

20

he didn't feel like eating it now. Why were lies so difficult? They were meant to be easy after the first one. And why, anyway, was he lying for George? Would George want him to lie to his father? He didn't know. He felt confused and sick. When his mother put the telephone down, she marched angrily over to him. 'Steven,' she said in her iciest voice, 'were you telling me the truth?'

'Yes,' Gishy said.

'Do you swear that this is the truth, that George Lewis was taken home?'

'Yes,' Gishy said.

'Well,' said his mother, 'he hasn't *been* home, so either something terrible has happened, or you're telling fibs.'

Gishy coughed again. He knew his face must be red.

'Something terrible must have happened, then,' he said weakly.

For Robert Lewis, these were probably the most terrible moments of his life. He was trying, however, to stay calm, to think clearly and to banish the pictures his mind kept making of George lying dead in a ditch, dead in the council tip, dead in the canal . . . He tried, also, to make sense of a feeling he had that George's disappearance was in some way connected with Anna. He dialled Serafima's number, but there was no reply.

Next, he telephoned the school, but the school was closed and no one answered. After this, he rang his old father, who was known as 'Norridge' and who lived on his own in a leaky old house in Hampshire. Norridge liked his grandson, George, a great deal more than he liked most people and he

21

was terribly upset to hear that he was missing. He swore on his life (all seventy-six years of it) that George wasn't with him and told Robert to telephone him again the minute he had any news. Robert agreed to do this and rang off. He sat down and sighed and thought for a while. Then, he went out.

He called at the houses of two neighbours where George sometimes played. No one had seen George since he'd left for school that morning. Robert hurried to his car and drove to the police station. His hands were shaking by now. When the sergeant at the desk offered him a cigarette, he took it, even though he'd given up smoking two years ago.

He was told to sit down. Then he was shown into a little bare room, a bit like a cell. A cup of tea was brought to him. In his quiet voice, he told a police sergeant called Murray that his son, George Roberto Lewis, aged eleven, height 5′ 1″, eyes brown, hair brown, was missing.

As he gave all the details (the clothes George was wearing, a description of his bike, the time he was last seen) he was also beginning to piece together the plan that Anna might have made and suddenly he found himself saying to Murray: 'It's just possible that my wife might have the boy and be planning to take him out of the country.'

Sergeant Murray looked up, surprised. 'Your wife? Now, you hadn't mentioned your wife, Sir.'

'We're . . . sort of separated,' Robert stammered. 'She's Italian . . . Sicilian, rather . . .'

'Her name, Sir?'

'What?'

'Your wife's name. What is it?'

'Anna.'

'Other names, Sir?'

'Other names? Oh yes. Anna, Valentina, Maria. *Please* find them!'

'We'll do our best, Sir. That's what we're here for. Now, can I have your wife's address, please?'

'She's staying with her friend. Smith. Serafima Smith,' Robert said distractedly. 'Haughly Road. Green door. I can't remember the number.'

Sergeant Murray wrote down the name Smith and sighed. He must have written this particular name more than a thousand times since he joined the police force. Up on the wall above Murray's head, there was a digital clock. Robert glanced up at it. It said 18.59.

Anna's eye was on the clock in Serafima's car. Though she'd made her plans well, she knew that time was desperately important. If there was any delay, if they missed the boat at Dover, then Robert would surely discover where they were and everything would go wrong.

But they were out of London now and driving fast on the motorway. Anna turned round and took George's hand and said: 'Now I can tell you where we're going. Tomorrow night we shall be in Aquilone.'

George smiled. 'I knew, Mamma,' he said.

'How did you know?'

'I thought about Nonna Violetta this morning. I nearly didn't go to school because I wanted to be there, in Aquilone.'

'Well, now you will be!'

It was a bit like magic, George thought. Thinking about Aquilone that very morning, wanting to be there. And now, being on his way. Tomorrow, Anna had said, he'd be there. He'd stand on Violetta's terrace and stare up at the fat stars. Perhaps he and Guido would sleep out on the mountain on canvas mats and wake up with the sunrise and eat melon for breakfast! This time, he decided, he would really become part of the family. He'd learn lots of Italian sentences. He'd help with everything, even the milking of the shit-bedraggled goats Guido hated. This time, he would forget England. He would forget his favourite things (like buying fudge ice cream at the Clapham *Dayville's*, like watching *Minder*, like going fishing with Gishy on Sundays) and even forget Garibaldi. He would forget his room. Altogether, he would forget his English home. It wouldn't be difficult. Would it? Only the thought of his father all alone in the house troubled him. It would be impossible to forget *him*. Every time there was a big meal and all the family chairs were pulled up to the big table on Aunt Sofia's terrace, he'd remember his father, alone with his frozen dinners. He rubbed his eyes. Why was life always only three-quarters good? Why was there always one quarter of something to make you feel sorry?

'Mamma,' he said suddenly, 'we should let Dad know where I am.'

Anna looked quickly at Serafima, who mumbled something in Italian, under her breath.

'Tomorrow,' said Anna. 'When we get to Catania, we can telephone.'

25

'But, I didn't leave a note or anything. He'll be so worried.'

'No, no. I don't think. I think your father will guess.'

'He might not. He might think I've been murdered or something.'

Again, Anna looked worriedly at Serafima. Again something was said quickly in Italian. Anna reached for George's hand. 'You do *want* to go to Aquilone, don't you?' she asked.

'Yes, of course I do.'

'Then you must understand this has to be our secret. Or some people will try to stop us. You must trust me, Giorgio.'

'I do trust you,' said George, 'I just don't want Dad to worry. If I've got to worry about him worrying, it's going to spoil everything.'

Anna shook her head. 'He won't worry. He will guess,' she said, 'eh, Serafima?'

'Oh yes!' said Serafima. 'He will know you are safe.'

George said nothing and stared out of the window at the fields and orchards of Kent. Only now did he remember Gishy. He felt relieved. Gishy had seen him leave. Gishy would telephone his father and tell him not to worry. And his father wouldn't try to stop them going to Aquilone, would he? He knew how much George liked it there.

George sat back, more comfortable now. He loved this fast, motorway driving. Nothing can stop us, he thought. We're speeding to the sea! At the white cliffs, England ends . . .

But the car was slowing. Up ahead, lorries and cars were

bunched in slow-moving lanes. Lights at the motorway edge were flashing. A police siren could be heard.

'Ah, no!' said Anna. 'What is *happening*?'

'*Non lo so*,' said Serafima. 'I don't know.'

They were almost at a standstill. Serafima started to crane out of the window, but all she could see was the long line of traffic.

'*Mamma mia!*' said Anna, running anxious, impatient hands through her hair. 'What is this, Serafima?'

Serafima shrugged. The traffic was stationary now.

'Go and ask someone of these drivers, Giorgio,' said Anna, 'go and ask what is happening.'

George got out of the car. They were in the outside lane. It was windy here, the wind coming off the sea. He could smell the sea in the wind and knew that they couldn't be far from it.

He ran up the road till he was level with a huge truck. It was the lorry men, George knew, who knew things about traffic. They had CB radios in their cabs and spoke to each other up and down the motorways. George banged on the door of the truck and a tanned face looked down at him.

'Excuse me,' said George, 'have you any idea why we're held up?'

'Yeh,' said the trucker, 'just got something on the CB. Caravan overturned. Blocking the slow lanes. 'Bout two miles on up.'

George thanked the lorry driver and repeated this news to Anna, whose face was now white and tense. 'Why are you so afraid, Mamma?' he wanted to ask. But he said nothing. He got back into the car and began to hum *Old Ab'ram Brown*.

3

The Wait

Robert Lewis left the police station and walked to his car. His hands were shaking and his legs felt tired, as if he'd been walking over a lonely desert for days and days.

'Don't do anything rash, Sir,' said Sergeant Murray, as they left the small, bare room. 'Go home and wait for our call. It's in our hands now.'

But Robert didn't go home. The thought of sitting and waiting by the telephone was too awful. Instead, he drove round to the street where Serafima lived and parked opposite her green front door. 'Let them be here . . .' he prayed.

He got out of the car and walked to the door and rang the bell. He waited. Through the coloured glass panes in the door, he could see light – the doorway to Serafima's kitchen. 'Let them be in there,' he said, 'let them be in there, having tea.'

No one came to the door. Robert rang the bell again, then banged on the door with his hands. Perhaps Anna was hiding from him. 'Anna!' he yelled. 'George!'

In the window of the house next door, he saw the curtains move and a neighbour's child stuck a fat face round them and stared at Robert sullenly. The stare of this child was horrible. Robert wanted to hit out at him, this gross boy, so safe in his parents' room! Why should this child be safe, when his own son was lost, or dead, even?

'Anna!' he called again. 'Serafima! Answer!'

But there was no movement inside the house. Robert stepped back into the street. The fat kid was blowing pink bubble gum on to the glass. Robert looked at all the cars parked by the little front gardens. He couldn't remember what car Serafima drove, or whether she and her husband even had a car. So what could he do now? Rush home to see whether, by some miracle, George had turned up. Robert Lewis didn't believe in miracles. I'll wait in the car, he decided. I'll wait half an hour.

The kid sucked the bubble gum back into his podgy mouth and left the window. Robert hoped that the taste of the sooty glass on the gum would be bitter and nasty.

It was while Robert was sitting uselessly in his car in front of Serafima's house that Giles Gish – Gishy's father – got home.

It was a warm evening and Giles Gish had been in a stuffy office all day. I'll do a spot of gardening before supper, he decided. So, after kissing his wife, he took off his creased office suit and tugged on his favourite clothes – some ancient, unfashionable flared jeans and a cotton shirt covered in palm trees. His son couldn't bear to look at his father wearing these ridiculous clothes. 'Dad,' he once said, 'you look like a dumbo. That shirt gives me diarrhoea.' But Giles Gish didn't care. The clothes were comfortable and comforting. He didn't mind if he looked ridiculous in them.

'Coming to help me tie up the sweet peas?' Giles called up to Gishy's attic bedroom. But there was no reply, so he went on down the stairs, happy in his silly clothes, and out of the back door and into his garden shed.

The shed was untidy, a jumble of garden tools, logs, empty boxes, sacks, bicycles and old discarded things like Gishy's pram all rusting away. But Giles Gish was so familiar with the shed that he knew exactly where and what everything was. Reaching for his hoe and a ball of twine, he noticed straight away a new and different arrangement of things. Gishy's bike was in its usual place, but behind this, sacks had been draped across something.

Giles put the twine down and lifted up one of the sacks. He saw the saddle of another bike, and behind the saddle a khaki school bag with a name inked in bold black writing between the buckles: GEORGE LEWIS. CLASS 3.

He was staring at the way this bike had been so carefully hidden and was pondering the reason for this, when a sound at the shed door made him turn. It was Gishy. The boy's face was frightened and pale. When he spoke, the words sounded confused: 'I hid it for George, Dad. Don't be angry. His mother came and they went off in a car, like a kind of kidnapping. I wrote the car number on my hand, but I don't know if this was helpful, or if not telling was best . . .'

'Okay, okay,' said Giles Gish kindly, 'no one's getting cross. Calm down, Steven.'

'But Mum's going to kill me!'

'No, she isn't. When did you last notice your mother killing anyone?'

'She will . . .'

'Don't be daft, Steve. Now, just tell me clearly what's been going on.'

He told. He had to stare at the stupid palm trees on his father's shirt to keep himself from feeling frightened by the seriousness of what he had done. He held up his hand and his father copied down the car registration number, OBJ 552W.

A little later, his mother poured herself a glass of white wine to stop herself saying unmotherly things to her lying son. The sun went in. Giles Gish started to feel chilly in his palm tree shirt. Mrs Gish poured more wine. Giles and Steven went into the kitchen and dialled Robert Lewis's number. I'm glad it's over, thought Gishy. Lies are awful.

Robert was in his kitchen when the telephone rang. The sound of it was like a fine chain being torn through his brain. He ran to the hall and snatched up the receiver.

'Hello? Hello?' for a brief, terrible second, there was a silence. Murray's found George, Robert thought. He's dead. He doesn't know how to tell me . . . 'Hello?' he yelled, again. 'Who is this?'

There was a cough at the other end of the line.

'Mr Lewis?' said a man's voice.

'Yes,' said Robert. 'Sergeant Murray?'

'No, this is Giles Gish here.'

'Who?'

'Giles Gish. Steven's father. I want to say how sorry I am about what's happened.'

'What's happened? What's happened?'

'Well, I feel very bad that you must have been worried about George. I gather you telephoned earlier and—'

'Yes?'

'Well, you were given the wrong information, I'm afraid. I really do apologise. We have George's bike with us. I'd like to come round and explain, if I may?'

'Where's George? Is he with you?'

'No. I'm afraid our young Steven's been playing amateur sleuth and has told us all quite a few fibs. We understand that he saw George leave school with his mother, in the car of a friend. We have the car number.'

Robert sat down. He found he couldn't speak. *He's safe. He's safe*, was all he could say to himself. *My son is safe.*

But then, in this moment of relief, while Giles Gish went on talking about how sorry he was and how sorry Steven was, Robert also began to see clearly what was happening. Anna had snatched George from school. At this very moment, they would be on a plane or on their way to a boat. If he let them get to Sicily, it could be months before he saw either of them again. Unless he got to Murray in time. This was his only hope. If Anna wasn't out of the country yet, the police might still be able to stop her.

'Forgive me,' Robert stammered to Giles Gish. 'I have to ring off now. There's an urgent call I must make.'

'*Cosa fare, cosa fare?*' wailed Anna in the front seat of the car. 'What can we do, Serafima?'

The traffic had been at a standstill for nearly half an hour now. George could imagine all the cars and lorries and

32

coaches piling up behind them, making a queue that would stretch for miles. Gishy had told him that one day all the traffic in London would come to a complete stop, nothing able to move in any direction, in any street. What would the drivers do then? Abandon their cars? Leave truckloads of bananas or chickens rotting and dying? George hated to think how complicated the world was. The world in England, at least, with all its traffic and crowds of people. In Aquilone, sitting and shelling beans with Violetta, you couldn't feel the world's complications. This, George thought, was probably the reason why Anna liked being there so much.

He could sense that his mother was near to tears. She also seemed scared. He wondered whether she was breaking some law or other by taking him away like this. When a police car sped up the stony centre section of the motorway, she looked away.

'What time is our boat?' George asked.

'7.15,' said Serafima.

'We can still make it,' said George.

'Maybe,' said Serafima, 'if we get a move on!'

She thumped the steering wheel. Up and down the lines of stationary traffic, people were getting out of their vehicles, walking up the road, coming back, checking their roof racks and their trailers, sighing, leaning on their cars, walking off again.

'These people are going on our boat too,' said George. 'You can tell.'

'Maybe,' said Anna.

'They are,' said George, 'you can tell by how worried they

are. So if there are all these people, the boat will have to wait.'

This seemed logical to George, but Anna shook her head. 'That's not the only point,' she said.

George was quiet. What did she mean, 'that's not the only point'? Did she mean that, with all this delay, someone – either his father, or the police – would try to stop them from getting on the boat? He stared out at the windy, sunny day. Suddenly, Aquilone seemed far, far away. He thought longingly of Violetta taking the clean sheets from the heavy wooden chest where she kept them and, with Aunt Sofia's help, pegging them out on her drying line in the sun.

But the traffic was moving at last. As the minutes ticked away on the car clock, the lorries and cars and coaches and caravans were inching up on the motorway.

Slowly, Serafima's car drew level with the scene of the caravan accident. The caravan, still attached to an over-turned Ford, lay across the slow lane, which had been cordoned off with cones. Men with a rescue truck were trying to right it. Further down the road, belongings were scattered: tins of food, folding chairs, suitcases, bedding. Police were still gathered here, two of them directing the traffic. Anna turned her face away.

George stared at the accident. He hated the way a tragedy could happen so suddenly; one minute you were going on holiday, the next you were lying in the road. He wondered if the people who'd been in the Ford were dead.

Anna's fists were clenched. 'Are we going to make it, Serafima?' she asked.

Serafima shrugged. What could she say? The time was

five to seven. They both knew that it was touch and go.

Fifteen minutes later, they pulled into the ferry quay. To Anna's relief, she saw that cars were stilll being loaded on to the boat and the gangways were still down. She leaned over and kissed her friend. '*Ciao*, Serafima. I will write.'

'*Ciao*, Anna. Hurry now.'

Anna and George scrambled out of the car. Anna grabbed two suitcases from the boot and gave George one of these to carry. It was heavy. Perhaps it was full of presents for Violetta, or perhaps they were going to stay in Aquilone for a long, long time. George wished he could have packed some clothes and books. What would he read while the grownups sat and talked? What would he wear when the clothes he was wearing were dirty? But he didn't really have time to wonder about this. Anna was tugging his arm.

'Hurry, Giorgio. Come on!'

Serafima stood by her car and waved. George waved back at her as they ran towards the waiting boat. 'Tell my father!' he shouted to her and he saw her nod.

Then Anna saw the policeman. He went into the little booth where tickets and passports had to be inspected. It's too late, she thought with dismay. Robert's discovered what I'm trying to do and the police are going to send us back. She wanted to sob. All her weeks of planning, all the money she'd spent on tickets, these were all going to be wasted. In less than an hour she'd be driving back to London – in a police car. In Aquilone, Violetta would unpeg the white sheets from the line and make up the beds they would never sleep in.

George, ahead of Anna now, was half running with the heavy suitcase. He turned to his mother and called: 'Come on, Mamma!' She hurried forward. As she did so, the policeman came out of the ticket booth and stood waiting for her.

4

South to Enzo

George leant on the rail of the upper deck of the ferry and stuck his face into the wind. The boat was in mid channel – sea all around. 'We're coming, Violetta!' he wanted to shout to the empty, windy sky. 'Nothing can stop us now!'

Anna sat back on a brown bench and closed her eyes. She loved boats. She didn't even mind rough weather. The rolling of the boat calmed and soothed her. The danger was past. The policeman at the booth had only stared at her but had said nothing. Clearly, he'd been waiting for someone else. So her plan had worked. Robert hadn't been able to stop her in time. She had run to the boat with her heart beating like an engine and ten minutes later the ferry had begun to move.

She felt sleepy. She wished the journey ahead wasn't so long, with so many stages: a train to Milan, then a flight to Catania, where Enzo would meet them in his ancient American car. She wished she could be in Aquilone now, lying in a tall wooden bed. Violetta would bend over her and kiss her goodnight, putting her papery lips on her forehead, just like when she'd been a child: '*Buona notte*, Anna . . .'

The reason why Anna Lewis had left home was her

longing to be back on the slopes of Mount Etna, where all her childhood had been passed. She longed to be there now because she'd had, for some time, this feeling, this premonition that her mother, Violetta, was dying. She didn't know exactly why she felt this. According to her letters, Violetta was well. She still cared for animals and tended her vegetable patch. She could still sing songs to little Filomena. Her life, in fact, was much the same as it had been since Vincente died – lonely at times, but busy and uncomplicated.

Her legs gave her pain. Each year, they seemed to bend inwards from the knee a little further. She couldn't go scrambling after her goats anymore. She tethered her goats now. If they pulled out the tether rings, one of the children had to go and find them.

Violetta joked that if her legs got worse, she'd have to lie in bed all day and let the family take care of everything. But no one believed her. Only Anna, far away in England, had this feeling that death was coming soon. And she wanted to spend one last summer with her mother, before it was too late. She'd tried to explain this very simply to Robert, but he hadn't understood.

Anna sighed when she remembered this and she stared up at the blue sky. High above the ship, gulls were circling.

In Aquilone, now, George's cousin Guido and his friend Fabio were chasing chickens. 'Kill me three fat ones,' Guido's mother, Sofia, had instructed, 'no miserable skinny things.'

They were hard to catch. They squawked. They took off

38

just as you thought you had your hands on them. They pecked. When you had them safely under your arm, you could feel the warmth of them, like the warmth of a dog or a cat. For a moment, feeling this animal warmth, you hesitated before wringing their sad necks. But then it was done. You thought of them roasted, dripping with oil, rubbed with garlic and salt. You felt hungry already . . .

Sofia and Violetta plucked the hens the boys killed, sitting on chairs in Sofia's yard. Two of Sofia's other children, Alfredo aged five and Anna-Maria aged six, ran about collecting the chicken feathers and putting them in a sack for bleaching. In Aquilone, nothing was wasted, certainly not feathers, from which the women made pillows and coverlets.

The sky above the women was still bright, but it was evening now and the sun no longer fierce. Behind them, obscured by Enzo's barn, was Etna, the volcano, lazily smoking as it did all day and all night. The women had lived under it all their lives. Eruptions and earthquakes had occurred in their lifetimes. You learned to live with these dangers. The mountain was cruel but the soil was good. You tried not to remember that the volcano could destroy everything you had, if it chose to one day.

'Well,' said Violetta, 'I'm glad Anna's coming. And Giorgio. This could be my last summer.'

'Don't say that, Mamma,' said Sofia, 'that's just foolish.'

Just then, Enzo came into the yard. Enzo was a large, untidy, hairy man with a big, round belly. His laugh was deep, as if it began, not in his throat, but in that fat belly of his. He loved large things: his wife's bosoms, for instance,

and his huge American car. He was glad all his babies were born big.

Enzo was waving a piece of paper in his hand. 'A letter from Mario Albertini!' he announced to the women. 'He's coming to Aquilone.'

'When?' asked Sofia, giving her hen a shake, to get rid of all the sticky feathers.

'Soon,' said Enzo. 'Read, read.'

He handed Sofia the letter. It told her that Mario Albertini was arriving in one week's time and that he looked forward to seeing all his dear friends again. Sofia read the letter quite a few times. Whenever Mario Albertini returned to Aquilone, it was a special day. He had left Aquilone as a very young man and gone to America. Now, he was rich. He owned a leather business. He was powerful and fierce, very kind to the people he loved, very cruel to those he didn't like. Everyone in Aquilone tried to stay in his good books. They invited him to their houses and he'd sit there smiling, showing off his teeth which had all been capped with gold.

'I wonder what presents Mario Albertini will bring for the children this time,' said Sofia.

'The children?' said Enzo. 'Never mind the children! What about presents for me?'

And he slapped his barrel chest and laughed.

George was very hungry. He'd only had an apple to eat at lunchtime. Otherwise, he'd eaten nothing since his tuna sandwich in the park. And so much had happened, it seemed to him as if two or three days had passed since then.

'I'm hungry, Mamma,' he told Anna.

But the boat was docking at Boulogne now. They were in France. 'You should have told me before,' said Anna. 'Never mind. We'll get you something on the train.'

She was nervous again, George could tell. They got off the boat, carrying the heavy cases, and joined a line of people waiting to go through customs. Two French policemen watched the new arrivals. They had guns on their hips.

'It's all right, Mamma,' George said to Anna, 'no one's going to stop us.'

'I hope,' said Anna. 'If we miss the Milano train . . .'

'We won't miss it,' said George.

'I hope. I hope,' said Anna.

Anna couldn't say the word 'hope' properly, George often noticed. She pronounced it as if it had a 'k' at the beginning: 'I *khope*'. Now, he wondered whether this was why Anna wanted to leave England – all her years of struggling with words like 'hope' that she couldn't say properly. It could be, he decided. Grownups were miserable for very peculiar reasons. Gishy's Gran was in a Home for Depressed People because she couldn't bear the way all the men in the government got fatter and fatter year after year. To see them on the telly made her feel disgusted, so she tried to diet for them. She got thinner and thinner and more and more miserable and now she was in this mad place in Sussex with a view of the sea. She only weighed six stone.

They were past the French police now, Anna holding tightly to George's hand. There was an hour's wait on the Milan train while cars were loaded on to long ramps at the back of it. George rather wished they had a car. Enzo's

Chevvy was so battered and uncomfy. George heard a lot of shouting about the cars in French. He thought of all the hundreds of languages there were in the world and wondered if he would ever know any of them. 'I *khope* I do,' he said to himself.

Then the train pulled out of Boulogne station. It was getting dark. George went in search of a buffet car, but the train didn't have one. It was just a line of sleeper cars and toilets, with lots of English and French families getting ready for the night.

George's stomach ached. He was weak with hunger, dying even. You could die if all you'd had for almost twelve hours was a tuna sandwich, an apple and a Bounty bar.

'Don't be silly!' said Anna, who was making up their little narrow bunks. 'Here.'

From her handbag, she fished out a half-eaten packet of wine gums. They tasted of lipstick and dust, but George lay down on his bunk and ate them all, and the train went thundering through the night.

It was late. The dog, Garibaldi, had peed on all his favourite flowers and was now trying to doze on his Happy Dreamer Doggybed. This was difficult, because Robert was screaming down the telephone to Serafima. He'd drunk three glasses of whisky and his head felt as if it had a whirling dervish inside it.

'Anna has no *right* to take George away!' he yelled. 'George is my son!'

'He's Anna's son too,' said Serafima, trying to stay calm.

'Anna left him. She left him and she left me.'

'Only for a while. She was a little sad . . .'

'And I don't want my son in the care of a sad person!'

'Oh, don't be so stupid, Robert.'

'And you had no business helping her. Can't you imagine how worried I've been?'

'I know. I'm sorry about that, Robert.'

'Whose side are you on?'

'Whose *side*? I'm not on any side . . .'

'Oh yes you are! You and Anna and all her fallaly . . .'

He meant to say 'all her family', but the whirling dervish in his brain was turning so fast, he couldn't get the proper words out.

'You're drunk, Robert,' said Serafima sternly. 'I'll talk to you tomorrow.'

'No, no!' yelled Robert. 'I'm getting on an aeroplane, now!'

'Don't be stupid,' said Serafima. 'I'm going to ring off now.'

'No! Don't you dare!' shouted Robert. But the line went dead.

Robert sat down in the kitchen. The room was spinning. He stared at the stupid dog, lying with its eyes open on the Happy Dreamer. George and Anna had both been very fond of this silly Garibaldi and now it was he, who had never liked it much, who was alone with it. Very slowly, Robert felt himself sliding on to the cold floor, where he went to sleep.

When George woke, the train was still moving, but there was pale white light at the edges of the blinds, and up and down the corridor a guard was shouting: '*Milan, dix minutes! Milano, dieci minuti!* Milan, ten minutes!'

George just had time to pull on his crumpled clothes and let Anna smear a wet flannel across his face, and then they were out on a station platform. It was cold. George had no jersey or coat and he shivered. They lugged the heavy cases to the station restaurant and queued for coffee and rolls. George ate five rolls and drank two cups of strong coffee and felt much better. Anna kept looking at her watch. 'Not long now,' she said.

But there was still more travelling to do. First, a taxi to the airport, then another long wait, and outside a grey drizzle began to fall. Then they were on the plane, and up above the clouds brilliant sunshine burst in on all the little plastic windows.

Anna felt like singing. Far away now seemed her fears. I'll forget England, she decided. Just for a while. I'll forget everything difficult. Life in Aquilone will be simple. I'll sit in the sun with Violetta. Nothing will bother me or upset me.

The *fasten seat belts* sign came on. They were coming down towards Catania. Way below them, Enzo would be waiting, with his dented, rusting Chevrolet. Enzo loved this car. He'd written, in a secret will, that when he died he wanted to be buried in it. He'd worked out that his grave would have to be sixteen feet long.

5

Aquilone

In the messy yard of Aunt Sofia's house, the baby, Filomena, was yelling in her pram.

'Guido!' yelled Sofia crossly. 'Get your fat feet out of this kitchen and go and rock the baby!'

It was a bright and brilliant day. The only cloud was the cloud of smoke on the volcano's tip.

Guido went out into the yard and began to rock his sister's pram. He rather liked babies. He liked the silly faces they made. He liked the fact that they had no manners: they got food all over their faces, they farted and burped, sitting on the laps of important guests. Sofia and Enzo often told Guido that he'd been 'a dreadful baby' and he wished he could have remembered that time.

Guido was happy today. He liked it when George came to Aquilone. It made his life more interesting. And he felt more important when George was around because George looked up to him. He taught George things, like how to ride Enzo's old donkey, how to nick tobacco leaves from their neighbour's barn and roll cigars with them, and how to make sundials.

Guido had a den high up in a rocky outcrop of the

mountain. He smoked here and made lizard traps. George was impressed by both these things and he made Guido feel cleverer and more grown-up than he was.

Guido stared at the yard. One side of it was like a scrap dump. There was the old car his father had abandoned when he bought the second-hand Chevvy, its seats yanked out, its tyres taken off. There was also an ancient plough and bits of a gas fridge Mario Albertini had once shipped all the way from America and which had exploded one day and blown a gigantic hole in Sofia's kitchen wall. There were rusty paint tins and pieces of fencing and broken tools and tiles and rubble.

In spring, weeds grew up and covered most of these things, but now, in the hot summer, the weeds were scorched and the sun glinted on the fridge handle and on the bits of chrome still left on the car. Guido knew this junk yard was ugly, but he liked it because he imagined that in America there were thousands of junk yards a bit like it. One day, Guido knew, he would go to live in America.

As Guido rocked the pram, his grandmother, Violetta, came into the yard, wearing her black Sunday dress, even though it was Saturday. (Since Vincente's death, Violetta always wore black clothes.)

'Guido,' said Violetta, 'I've lost my little goat, Augustina. Go and find her for me.'

'I'm meant to rock the pram, Nonna.'

'Leave the pram. Go and find the goat.'

The moment Guido took his hand off the pram, Filomena began crying again. From the house, Sofia called out: 'Guido! What did I tell you to do? Can't you rock that pram as you're told, for once?'

'Go, go!' said Violetta.

Guido shrugged and ran out of the yard. Grownups, he thought. Always getting errands out of you. This was partly why he'd built his den. He hid from the errands there.

He started to run up the path that led to Violetta's house and on up the slopes of the mountain itself. It was a path made by the feet of men and animals. Generations of people and goats had made it. Many of the people, like Vincente, now lay under the marble tombs of the Aquilone cemetery. And as for the goats, hundreds of these had been the Sunday dinners of those same dead villagers. Guido thought about this. He was glad he was a boy and not a goat or a lizard to be killed and eaten. He and Fabio had had a lizard feast once. Lizard meat tasted like chicken. If I was a cannibal, Guido decided, I'd eat babies.

Just as Guido set off in search of Violetta's goat, Enzo's car was beginning the twisty climb up to Aquilone.

Most of the way from Catania, Enzo and Anna had talked to each other in the Sicilian dialect and George had begun to feel left out and nervous. Till he'd spent some time with them, Anna's family always seemed like strangers to him. Even Guido. The first few hours with him were always difficult. And there in the back of Enzo's car, George had a pang of missing Gishy and his other friends. Maybe he was here for ever now and Anna would never let him go back to England. He had a sick feeling in his stomach.

'Hey!' said Enzo, turning his big neck round and smiling at George. 'How's the schooly?'

'Oh, okay,' said George.

'You toppy?'

'What?' said George.

'Toppy the class, you?'

'No.'

'*Non*? Why you not toppy?'

George shrugged. He remembered suddenly that if he was going to stay in Aquilone, this would mean going to Guido's school. He'd seen this school. It seemed like a poor, run down place, grey and dull. He didn't want to go there. He glared at Enzo. Enzo grinned.

'Oh you don't take any notice! I'm joke about toppy. Enzo don't give any damn you toppy or not. Hey! You know what we eat tonight? Some wild pig. You like?'

'I don't know,' said George, feeling sicker than ever.

'Yes, you like this, darling,' said Anna comfortingly.

'I've never had it before,' said George.

'Well, now you have it!' said Enzo. 'I kill this wild boar with my own hand, you know?'

Enzo was a bit like Fabio – he loved lying.

'Did you?' said George. But he tried not to think about eating wild pig. He had one sudden longing – to be at home in London.

On Moses Friday, George Lewis sits in a London park and wishes he was in Aquilone.

The next day, George Lewis finds himself driving to Aquilone and wishes he was back in London.

Life is indeed peculiar.

But George had no time to think about this. The car was pulling up outside Aunt Sofia's yard, Enzo tooting the horn. In a second, Sofia was there, holding out her arms, and followed a moment later by Violetta. When George saw his grandmother, he got out of the car and ran to her. With her, he didn't feel shy or afraid. She held him to her with one thin arm round his neck and when he looked up at her, he saw there were tears of joy running down her face.

'Giorgio!' she said. 'Now you stay with Nonna!'

That evening, as the supper table on Sofia's terrace was laid, as vegetables were being salted and potatoes roasted and the wild boar stew was simmering in wine, Guido came back with Violetta's goat. It was dead. It had fallen, Guido said, into a gully from some slippery lava rocks. Its head was crushed. Guido was smeared with its blood.

Sofia told Guido to put the dead goat in Violetta's shed and to go and wash before he said hello to Aunt Anna and Cousin Giorgio. When he came back (with the blood washed from his hands, but not from his clothes) he sat down by George and nudged him. 'Tomorrow we go to the den. You come?'

'Yes,' said George, feeling better now and hungry for the meal, 'that's great.'

Sofia had spread her best linen cloth across the big table. Around this, the family gathered, as the sky behind the volcano slowly deepened to red. Enzo said a long but hurried grace. Sofia tied napkins round the children's necks. The jug of wine passed from hand to hand, Guido pouring a full glass for George. Then came the heavy plates on to which Sofia ladled her stew. Enzo slapped his stomach and even Violetta moistened her lips with pleasure. And as for Anna, George noticed that his mother's eyes were shining with happiness.

From the terrace where they sat, you could look down on the main part of Aquilone, the church tower, the cemetery, the pink roofs of the houses. And, far beyond this, you could see the sea. George stared at all this. It was beautiful. He only felt sorry that his father, all alone with his frozen dinners, couldn't be there to see it.

People and animals all woke at dawn in Aquilone. Up at Violetta's house, her prize cockerel, Peppi, strutted about the yard, waking the hens, and the hens scratched in and out of the goat pens, and the bleating of the goats woke Violetta.

When George woke, he knew exactly where he was. His room was small, whitewashed, with a scrubbed wooden floor. On the wall above his narrow bed there was a crucifix, nothing else, no posters like he had at home, no mobiles or cards or swimming certificates, just the little ivory Jesus on the cross.

By eight o'clock (the time he usually got up in London), George had eaten his breakfast of bread and coffee and Guido was there, carrying something in a sack over his broad shoulders. 'We go to the den,' he said to George.

'Guido!' called Violetta. 'If you're going up the hill, you can take the goats today. Take them up high.'

'Yes, Nonna,' said Guido.

'Come into the kitchen,' the old woman called, 'I'll give you some food for you and Giorgio.'

So Guido and George set off, the scraggly goats scampering ahead of them. Violetta had given them long sticks with which to thwack the goats when they strayed. George carried their meal in an old string bag: heavy white bread, smoked ham, two fat peaches and a flask of water.

Guido walked fast, used to the heavy climb. George began to puff and pant. He looked enviously at the big muscles in Guido's legs. Guido turned and waited for him to catch up, switching the skinny rumps of the goats to keep them near him. But this was difficult. The goats could smell the fresher, richer grass further up. They wanted to be there.

'You go on!' George shouted to Guido. 'I'll follow.'

Half an hour later, with the goats spread out, quietly grazing, George recognized the rock formation behind which Guido's den was hidden. He was sweating. He took a long drink from the water flask. When he looked up again, he saw Guido standing on a jutting rock and waving to him. Beside Guido was another, taller figure, not waving, but staring coldly. It was Fabio. George's heart lurched. Though he didn't want to admit it, he was afraid of Fabio. He was only twelve, but he had a man's face already. He knew how to threaten you. He didn't seem afraid of anything.

George paused. Should he go back and spend the day with Anna and Violetta? He felt silly and weak. Go on, you baby, he told himself, don't be such a coward. So he climbed on up. Sweat ran into his eyes. It was still early morning, but the sun was fierce. A pebble hit George on the shoulder. It had been thrown at him by Fabio. He ignored it. Guido jumped down from his rock and laughed.

George followed Guido and Fabio in through the 'door' of the den and sank down in the shade of the massive rocks which formed its walls. It was a weird place. Guido had furnished it from the junk pile in Enzo's yard. Planks had been slung across two rusty paint tins to form a low seat. A rat-bitten and stained mattress was laid out in one corner. A table had been built out of heavy, flat stones.

'Okay?' said Guido to George, who was wiping the sweat off his face.

'Yes,' said George.

'*Bene*. So now we get sticks. We make a fire.'

'Fire?' asked George. 'Isn't that dangerous? I thought you said you weren't meant to make fires in the summer.'

'No. Not dangerous today,' said Guido. 'Come.'

Sticks and twigs weren't hard to find. There was dry gorse and ilex scrub all around and, lower down, some olive trees that had died.

Guido and Fabio, who said nothing to George, squatted down and made a ring of large stones. Bundles of sticks and handfuls of parched olive leaves were put inside this. Then Fabio produced what looked to George like a very expensive cigarette lighter and he held the little flame to the leaves. They soon caught and small tongues of fire began to spring up.

Now they went to look for larger pieces of wood, wrenching dead boughs from the olive trees. When they had a big armful each, they carried these up to the fire which was burning well now. Fabio laid the logs on and the heat from the fire grew.

Guido then fetched the sack he'd brought with him and Fabio and he bent over it, whispering. George was told to watch over the fire. He stared at it. He wished Fabio wasn't here. He knew Fabio didn't like him.

Smoke from the fire now rose way above the rock walls of the den. It was like a tiny imitation of the smoke that came from the volcano a few miles above them. George wondered if it could be seen in the village, by Violetta and Anna, shelling beans.

George turned to see Guido carrying something red towards him. Guido was holding it at arm's length and he and Fabio were walking slowly, stiffly, as if they were in a procession.

'What's that?' asked George.

Guido didn't reply, but came to the fire and bent down and on to the fire threw the bleeding parcel in his hands. George gasped. It was a goat's head. As the fire singed the hair, a bitter smell came from it and the eyes in the poor head began to bulge and melt.

George looked away. Fabio and Guido were kneeling now and stretching out their hands to the fire and murmuring some incomprehensible words, their eyes tightly shut.

'What are you saying?' whispered George.

After a moment, Guido opened his eyes and looked sternly at George. 'You don't tell no one,' he said.

'I promise,' said George.

'We make a *sacrificio*.'

'A sacrifice?'

'Yes.'

'Why, Guido?'

'To the *vulcano*. To make her quiet.'

'But why a goat's head?'

Guido consulted quickly with Fabio before replying. Then, struggling with the English words, he said: 'When the fire come from the *vulcano* one time, many goats burn. So the old women decide, the *vulcano* like to eat goat, you see?'

'Sort of,' said George.

'*Bene*. We make a goat sacrifice. Now the *vulcano* is quiet.'

'Do you believe this, Guido?'

Guido looked down for a moment, but then he said: 'The *vulcano* is get angry. In the spring there are some small earthquakes.'

'Are these a bad sign?'

'Yes. A bad sign. So we make this *sacrificio*.'

George stared at the horrible, burning head for a moment and then he remembered Guido coming back the evening before and telling Violetta her goat had fallen. 'Did you kill Nonna's goat, Guido? Or did it really fall?'

'No,' said Guido. 'I kill.'

6

The Man from America

George and Guido stayed on the mountainside till the sun started to go down. The goat's head was burnt to its skull. When the fire cooled, they pulled the skull out of the ashes and buried it in the rocky earth.

At midday, when the sun was at its hottest, Fabio had gone off. Fabio's father was a car mechanic. From two till seven every day, Fabio had to help his father with the cars. He was the eldest of five children and his future was mapped out already: he'd become a mechanic like his father. He would probably live and die in Aquilone and never once leave the island of Sicily.

Guido, however, had other plans for himself. During this hot day on the mountain, he told George about these plans. Guido's godfather was Mario Albertini, the man who owned the leather business in America, the man with the gold teeth. This was fortunate. In Sicily, godfathers did special favours for their godchildren. The favour Guido was going to ask was a job in Mario Albertini's leather business.

'In America?' asked George, surprised.

'Yes,' said Guido. 'I speak English good already, no?'

'You'll leave Uncle Enzo and Aunt Sofia and everyone?'

'Yes. I leave them.'

'When?'

'In two years.'

'When you're fourteen?'

'Yes. At fourteen I get work.'

George thought about this. At fourteen, he'd be starting his O-level course – if he went back to his London school. But supposing he didn't go back? If he went to Guido's school here, would they make him leave in three years' time and find work? He knew his father wouldn't want this to happen. His father nagged him about doing well enough at school to get to university. But what about Anna? She'd never had a good education. She'd worked in the china shop where Robert had met her since she was fifteen. She sometimes said, to Robert's irritation, that she thought education wasn't necessary. 'Love and hard work, that's all you need,' she'd say. And Robert would sigh. 'Anna,' he'd complain, 'sometimes you say absolutely idiotic things.'

One thing George learnt on this hot day was the importance of Mario Albertini. He was very rich. No one in Aquilone had ever made as much money as Mario Albertini, and there were rumours that he owned other, secret businesses, not just the leather business. But no one dared to ask him about these because they wanted him to go on coming back to Aquilone with presents for everyone and doing things for the village. Last time he'd come, he'd rebuilt the cemetery gates that were falling down. The time before, he'd paid for six miles of piping to be laid, so that Aquilone could be connected to the mains water supply. He had enemies, of course. 'If you are rich and powerful, you make enemies,' said Guido. The Capelli family were enemies of Mario Albertini and they'd left Aquilone, where they'd once owned a big house, because of him.

'Why?' asked George.

But Guido shrugged his shoulders. 'Some business,' he said. 'Someone dead. These families were big rivals.'

Now, Mario Albertini was coming back. The family would give a feast in his honour, of course – he expected this. Sitting at Sofia's table, his gold teeth would glint and flash as he smiled at everyone. The children – including Guido – would stare at these expensive teeth, feeling peculiar, wearing the baseball caps Mario Albertini always brought them. He'd chatter in English, teaching the children English words. His wife was American, blonde and pretty. She hardly even came to Sicily, but whenever she did, she made Sofia feel poor and plain.

'I won't like Mario Albertini,' said George.

'Why?' asked Guido.

'I don't like the sound of him.'

'Everyone likes him,' said Guido.

'Except the Capelli family,' said George.

Guido was silent for a moment. Then he said sadly: 'I hope I can go to America. This place is no good.'

It didn't seem 'no good' to George that day. It seemed wild and exciting. After Fabio had gone, they ate their lunch. The goat bells tinkled, the sky was a fantastic blue. George longed to go to the sea. Perhaps Enzo would take them all in his Chevvy one day.

After eating his bread and ham, George felt sleepy. He lay

down on the old mattress and dozed and he had a strange dream about Mario Albertini. He dreamed this man arrived wearing a broad-brimmed hat, like a gangster. Under the hat was not his face, but the goat's head, its eyes bulging, its skin charred from the fire. George yelled to Anna, to Violetta, to Guido: 'Look! Look at his face!' But they just stared blankly. They didn't seem to notice that anything was wrong.

The arrival, a few days later, of Mario Albertini was remarkable.

He came in a big, black shiny car. It was a Cadillac, but it looked like a funeral car, George thought.

It was early evening and Guido and George were giving little Filomena a bath in the big tin tub Sofia used for clothes washing. They'd put the tub on the front terrace, so they were the first to see the car arrive.

George watched Guido. The minute he saw whose car it was, Guido dried his hands and stood up. He stood to attention, like a boy scout. Then, out of the house came Enzo and Sofia.

'Get glasses!' Enzo shouted at his wife. 'Get the good wine!'

So Sofia scuttled back inside, whipping off her cooking apron, patting her hair. And Enzo then turned to George, who was holding little slippery Filomena in the bath water, and yelled: 'You take this away. Quick, quick!'

George looked up for Guido to help him, but Guido was standing stiff and straight, his eyes fixed on the road. It was almost as if a spell was being cast, a spell that made Guido behave like a boy scout, made Enzo bad-tempered, made Sofia ashamed of the way she looked. Feeling uneasy, George picked up the dripping baby and wrapped her in a towel. He couldn't hold Filomena *and* move the tub. He looked at Enzo, but Enzo too was staring straight at the road.

He went inside with Filomena and handed her – she was crying now – to Anna, who was waiting silently in the dark of the kitchen. Then he went out again and began to pull the heavy tub round to the side of the house, out of sight. At that moment, the black Cadillac whispered to a stop beside Enzo's Chevvy, making the Chevvy look even more awful and dilapidated than it was. A tall man got out. He was wearing a wide-brimmed hat, just like the hat in George's dream.

When he'd pulled the bath tub out of sight, George waited in the shadow of the wall, where it was cool. He could hear Enzo and Guido and Mario Albertini talking in Sicilian and laughing and slapping each other on the back. Then he heard Enzo call: 'Sofia! Anna! *Veni!*'

And he peered out from the shadow to see Sofia and his mother lining up politely in front of Mario Albertini and holding out their hands for him to kiss. George stared at Anna. Much shorter than this tall stranger, she was now gazing sweetly up at him. And he was handsome, George recognised, much more handsome than his father. He had a brown, hard-seeming face and curly grey hair. He wore a white suit. He seemed a bit like a film star.

The younger children, Alfredo and Anna-Maria, came running out now. Little Anna-Maria was naked except for a

pair of grubby knickers, and George saw Sofia pull the child to her roughly and shake her head, apologising to Signor Albertini. But he didn't seem to mind Anna-Maria's grubby knickers. He held out his arms to her and lifted her up and smacked kisses on her cheek. Then, still carrying the little girl, he led the whole family towards his car. 'Presents!' he announced. 'Presents for you all.'

It was like a funny kind of Christmas Day then. The family came in a line to the table on the terrace, where Sofia had hurriedly set out her best glasses and two bottles of good wine, and they all sat down and started to unwrap the gifts Mario Albertini had brought them.

As usual, the children had baseball hats, which they put on, but George noticed that Guido looked a bit disappointed with his. There was no present for Anna, but Sofia had been given a smart leather handbag, which she began to caress with her rough hands, then handed it to Anna and Anna caressed it with her hands too. Enzo's present was the largest. Out of the big parcel, he took a huge pair of shiny shears. 'From Sears-Roebuck,' Mario Albertini announced. 'Wonderful quality.'

Enzo examined the shears and looked puffed up and pleased like a big bullfrog. Sofia poured wine for all the grownups and they all raised their glasses and toasted Mario Albertini, who took off his horrible hat and pressed it to his chest, while he made an odd little bow. He smiled and smiled and George could see his mother smiling and smiling back.

George turned away. He felt strange – rather hot and sick. He dreaded the moment when someone would remember him and call him over. He didn't want to shake Mario Albertini's hand. He didn't want to sit there at the table. He rubbed his eyes. The arrival of this stranger from America had upset him in a way that he couldn't express. Keeping to the back of the house, out of sight of the terrace, he began to make his way up the hillside to Violetta's house.

Half way there, thinking he was safe now, he met Violetta on her way down. She, too, had seen the American car, so then she'd put on a clean black dress and stuck all the loose pins back into her wispy hair, and come hurrying down the hill on her poor painful legs. She looked pleased and excited. 'Such wonderful presents Signor Albertini bring to Nonna. You come and see, Giorgio.' She took George's hand. He wanted to resist. He wanted to say, 'Don't go, Nonna. Hide me in your house till that man's gone.' But he couldn't say these things. He couldn't spoil Violetta's excitement with his own fears. So he let his hand be held and he walked back with his grandmother towards the house.

Mario Albertini was invited to stay for dinner, of course. While the men drank and smoked and talked on the terrace, the women and children worked to make the dinner as good as possible. A smoked ham and a big cheese wrapped in muslin were fetched from the larder. Guido and George were sent down to Signor Maretti, the butcher, to buy veal. Anna made a thick tomato sauce with fresh basil leaves and Sofia mixed flour and eggs for fresh pasta.

By this time in the day, George was usually very hungry. On this peculiar night, however, with the dusk beginning to settle silently on the village of Aquilone, he didn't feel hungry at all. In fact, the sick feeling he'd had earlier wouldn't leave him and he had to wait outside in the street while Guido went into the smelly Maretti shop.

He felt hot, too, and a bit dizzy. When they returned with the veal, it was like a furnace in Sofia's kitchen and George felt as if he was going to suffocate. No one noticed his distress. The women were too busy. Outside on the terrace, Enzo was getting drunk and laughing his big belly-laugh and slapping the table top and starting to talk in English, which he loved to do when he'd had a lot of wine. 'America bloody fantastic!' George heard him say. 'My bloody children all go to America one day!'

George knew that Sofia, who was a very religious person, hated it when Enzo swore, but this evening she was too busy to notice, or else she didn't understand English swear words. Anna heard them, but she only laughed and said to George: 'Uncle Enzo is very happy tonight, eh, Giorgio?'

George nodded. Someone thrust a colander of beans into his lap to shell and he thought of the way Anna loved to sit in the sun with Violetta and shell beans. But this was the last thought he had before he felt himself falling and falling, falling and falling down a big, echoing green well, into darkness.

He had fainted. He was lying on the kitchen floor. Nonna Violetta was holding a little bottle to his nose. He could see the round faces of Alfredo and Anna-Maria gazing down at him, and above them, rather indistinct, Anna's face. He could feel beads of sweat on his forehead. He'd been terribly hot. Now, he was ice cold. He wanted to speak, to ask Anna to carry him to bed, but he found he couldn't speak. Somewhere in the distance, Filomena was crying and George was aware of the commotion all around him.

Violetta helped him to sit up. Anna knelt now and took his hand in hers. Together, they helped him to stand. Alfredo and Anna-Maria were going round picking up the beans that George had dropped. Then, he walked between Anna and Violetta along the passage to Guido's room and they laid him down on the hard bed and covered him. Anna sat on the bed and held his hand. Though he felt very weak, George smiled at her and she smiled back. Since we came to Sicily, George thought, she seems to smile more often.

He slept quite soon. Some time later, he woke up and he was alone. He lay in the dark and listened. Outside on the terrace, the party was going on noisily. Everyone sounded happy. There was a lot of chatter and laughter and clinking of glasses and rattling of spoons and dishes and plates. George felt very ill, he now realised. He felt burning inside, yet cold on his skin. He tried to work out what was happening to him. Had Mario Albertini understood that he was his enemy, not his friend as all the family were his friends? Had he seen this in the first moment when Nonna Violetta had pushed him forward to shake the man's hand? So powerful had he seemed, this godfather of Guido, that George found himself wondering whether it could be this power that had made him ill. He'd felt well this morning, now he felt as if he was dying.

At about midnight, Violetta came in and sat by George and stroked his forehead. Her hands were gentle and cool. She smiled at him and he felt calmer. How much he loved

Nonna! But then he thought, how old she is, and lined and sad. And old, sad people seem so near to death. He felt tears start in his feverish eyes. Violetta saw them at once.

'Tell Nonna why you cry, my boy.'

George shook his head.

'Tell Nonna, Giorgio.'

'No, Nonna.'

'Then you sleep, my chicken. Tomorrow you are well again.'

George nodded. In the quiet and dark of the room, a tiny fieldmouse stuck its nose out from under Guido's wardrobe. Violetta shooed it out into the passage, then she turned to George and smiled. 'When Nonna dies,' the old woman said, 'she become a busy mouse, to watch over all her children.'

7

Ghosts and Rhubarb Leaves

George had sunstroke. At night, he felt as if his body was on
fire. In the day, the light in his room hurt his eyes. His head
ached and he was thirsty all the time.

Sofia made him drinks from the lemons she'd harvested
on her own land that spring. Guido brought him a flat,
smooth stone he'd found near his den. The stone was always
cool, he said. You put it in your hand or on your forehead
and it cooled you down. And it did.

Violetta picked him cherries from the tree outside her
verandah. Anna sat with him and told him stories about her
childhood, when Nonno Vincente had been alive.

Several days passed. It was July now. No rain fell. The
heat that buzzed on the hillside was as fiery as the heat on
George's brow. And Mount Etna was angry, Guido told
him. She was smoking a lot. The smoke was black, which
meant she was in a bad mood. 'What about the sacrifice?'
George asked. But Guido only shrugged.

'Maybe we have to make another one,' he said.

One night during his illness, George had a nightmare
about his father. He dreamed that Robert had cut off three
of his toes and had mashed them up and put them into a

little plastic tray, like a TV dinner. He was about to eat them – eat his own toes! – when George and Anna walked into the kitchen of their London house. 'Oh,' said Robert, 'so you've come back?' And he set the terrible meal aside.

The next morning, George remembered the dream and began a letter to his father.

Dear Dad, (he wrote)
I hope you are well. How is Garibaldi? How is your Boomerang Plan? I have got sunstroke. My temperature was about a thousand one night. I miss you. A man came here I hated and then I was ill. Mamma is fine. She's telling me about when she was little.
    I don't know if you're going to come here or not. I am going to smuggle this letter to you. Is my bike okay?
Love from George
PS. I want you to come here.

He hid the letter under his pillow. He knew that Anna had written to Robert, telling him not to follow them to Sicily, and she didn't seem to want to talk about London or their life there. When George had asked her what was going to happen about school, she had just turned away. 'I don't discuss any of these things yet,' she said sternly.

So the future was confused. Part of George was struggling to belong in Aquilone and doing rather well at it. But another part of him couldn't help missing his school and his friends and his father. He wished he could divide himself up, so that he could be in both places at the same time.

A day or two later, he was allowed to get dressed. Sofia brought him a battered, floppy hat of Enzo's and told him to wear this whenever he went out. He put it on and it almost covered his eyes. Wearing the hat, he carefully transferred his letter from under his pillow to his trouser pocket. They were Guido's trousers, very worn and old. With these on, and Enzo's hat, he felt like a tramp. And he felt thin in these garments – a skinny ragamuffin.

He looked around for Guido down at Sofia's house. He would tell Guido about his letter and Guido would get the right stamp for him at the post office. But Guido had gone, Sofia told George proudly, to work for Mario Albertini. He was doing useful jobs for him, like watering his grass and washing his car. He was doing them as favours. Later, Signor Albertini would repay these favours by giving Guido 'proper' work in America.

It was quiet in Sofia's house. Filomena was sleeping. Enzo was in his olive orchards, where the olives were ripening. Alfredo and Anna-Maria were with him, helping to collect every precious olive that had fallen. Nothing in Aquilone could be wasted. This family was poor, George understood this now. Everything produced here was scarce and precious.

Though he was still a bit wobbly on his legs, after his illness, George decided he would walk to the next village, Monte Passerino, with his letter and buy a stamp at the post office there. He set out. One problem was, he hadn't been able to find an envelope in the house and hadn't dared to ask for one. He was hoping he could buy one, or find an envelope at the post office. He had a few coins in his pocket, superstitious small change Violetta had given him to help him get well. He didn't know whether this was enough money for an envelope and a stamp.

He was barely out of Aquilone, on the steep road down to Monte Passerino, when he began to feel very thirsty. He knew that somewhere on this road was a drinking fountain. He hoped he'd get to it soon. He pulled Enzo's hat further on his head to shield him from the burning sun, and trudged on. He could see the roofs of Monte Passerino now. They looked a long way off.

At intervals along the road, there were strange shrines built into the rock. Propped up in them were photographs of people who had died and they were decorated with ugly plastic flowers. George found them very odd. Were people actually buried here, instead of in the cemetery? If so, why had they chosen to lie by the roadside? Had they been killed by cars or trucks? Had they died in those exact places?

George stopped at one of the shrines and read out the name of the man who had died: Giovanni Capelli. He stared at the face. He'd heard that name, Capelli, before. He knew there was something important about it, but he couldn't remember what.

Just beyond the Capelli shrine, he came to the drinking fountain. The water was clear and icy – not like the drinking fountain at school, where the water was luke-warm and seemed to taste of germs. George drank for several minutes and splashed water on to his face. In the distance, now, he could see the sea. He thought longingly of this. But the family hardly ever went to the sea. They said the sea was for the tourists and the fishermen. They were hill people and they had to stay on their hill and work.

When he came at last to Monte Passerino, it seemed like a deserted place. Dogs lay about, sleeping in the sun. Some old men sat on chairs on the pavement and stared at the empty street. George noticed that quite a few of the houses were half built, with steel rods and girders sticking out of them and dark spaces where there should be windows. It was a sad place. He was glad he didn't live here. He fingered the letter in his pocket. His father seemed so far, far away. It was almost impossible to imagine a letter that started its journey in this poor village ever ending up in Clapham!

George found his way to the post office. There was no one inside it except one post office employee. George went boldly up to the counter and said: '*Un francobollo. Per Inghilterra. Per favore.*' The post office worker looked at him out of large, sleepy eyes. Everyone in this village seemed sleepy. It was the sun and the dead people on the road, George decided.

George paid for his stamp and went to a side counter, set out with pens and blotters. The stamp had taken all the money he had. But underneath the counter was a large, tin waste paper basket half full of papers. George knew that this was probably his only hope of finding an envelope. He squatted down and began to rummage through it. He felt stupid. He was glad Gishy couldn't see him like this, frantically searching for an envelope to steal, looking like a slum child in his battered hat.

There were some envelopes in the bin, but they were all torn. He couldn't send his letter in a torn envelope: it would never get there. He pulled out his letter and looked at it. Then he shrugged, folded it carefully and wrote the name and address on one of the folded sides: Mr Robert Lewis, 23 Cramphorn Gardens, Clapham, London SW11, England.

He stuck his stamp on the letter and dropped it into the post box. Would it ever get to London? Do letters without envelopes ever get to anywhere? George didn't know. He walked out into the sunshine knowing only that he had done his best.

He got out of Monte Passerino as quickly as he could and started to climb the steep road back up to Aquilone. At a turn in the road, he noticed, for the first time, some iron gates, large and ornate, leading on to a stony driveway. He stopped. The grandeur of the gates made George certain that they led to a grand house, and this was odd, because apart from Mario Albertini's house, there were no grand houses in Aquilone. He held on to the gates and stared down the driveway. Dry weeds grew in the centre of it. It seemed neglected, as if no one walked down it anymore.

Then, from the shadow of the cypress trees that bordered the drive, George saw a man step out on to the path and walk towards him. The man was about forty, dressed very formally in a dark suit, and there was something oddly familiar about him.

George held tight to the iron gates and watched. Nearer and nearer the man came. He was smiling. George knew the man was going to come and talk to him. For some reason he felt that, out of politeness, he should take off his battered hat, so he reached up and took it off and felt the sun blaze down on his head. He blinked. The sun hurt his eyes. He looked up again and the man had gone.

George rubbed his eyes, then put the hat back on. The drive was deserted. This was strange. He'd been so certain that the man was going to talk to him. He'd had such a friendly smile. George waited, but he didn't return, so he walked on up the road.

Just round the corner, he came to the Capelli shrine and went up to it, to have another look at the photograph. Then George felt cold. He put his arms round himself and stared. The dead man in the picture was the man he'd just seen on the driveway – the same smile, the same small moustache, the same dark striped suit. He had seen the ghost of Giovanni Capelli!

He turned away and started to run. He puffed and panted. His legs were weak and his heart was beating so fast, it felt as if it was going to burst. Because by now, he'd remembered where he'd heard the name 'Capelli'. Guido had said this name. It was this family who were the enemies of Mario Albertini! And George now felt certain – as certain as he was that his name was George Lewis – that it was Mario Albertini who had killed Giovanni Capelli.

He ran on. He felt frightened and confused. When he reached Sofia's house, he wanted to go tearing into her kitchen and shout: 'I saw a ghost! I saw the ghost of Giovanni Capelli!' But he was afraid to do this. He was afraid Mario Albertini might be sitting right there at Sofia's table. My enemy, George thought. Giovanni Capelli knew that he's my enemy. That's why he appeared to me.

But there was no one in Sofia's kitchen. On the stove, a thick soup was simmering. It smelled good, but George didn't feel hungry at all.

Guido returned in the late afternoon. He seemed happy and very pleased with himself. He suggested they go up to the den for a while, and George agreed. He had to tell *someone* about the ghost. Perhaps he would risk telling Guido?

They were about to set out when Sofia came to find them. She was holding Filomena, who had been yelling all afternoon. Sofia seemed anxious, near to tears. 'Guido,' she said, 'help me. You're so good with Filomena. You rock her to sleep for me.'

Guido took the baby. Her little face was bright red and tear-stained. 'I think she must be ill, Guido,' said Sofia, 'shall we send for the doctor?'

'No,' said Guido calmly, 'you have a little rest, Mamma. I'll take care of her. We'll go for a walk.'

'Be careful, Guido. Don't take her far.'

'Don't fret. We'll look after her.'

Sofia gave Guido a kiss on the top of his thick mop of curly hair and went off to lie down on her bed for a while. 'Come on,' said Guido to George.

They put Filomena in her pram and started to push her up the path. She was still crying and flailing her arms and legs. Her antics only amused Guido. He started to talk to her and laugh at her, and after a few moments, she stopped crying and lay still and looked at him.

They were near Enzo's vegetable plot. 'You hold the pram,' Guido told George. And George watched Guido scamper across Enzo's lines of peas and beans to a big clump of rhubarb, its gigantic leaves like big green bonnets. Guido took out a penknife from his pocket and cut several of these leaves and ran back with them. It grew in shade, this rhubarb, and the leaves were cool.

Guido covered Filomena tightly with the pram sheet and

then pressed the big leaves all round and over her body. Her pink face looked like a little caterpillar's head coming out of a green chrysalis.

George remembered his school nature studies. 'They're poisonous, those leaves,' he said.

'No,' said Guido.

'Yes, they are,' said George, 'we were told this at school.'

'No,' said Guido again. 'Only if you eat.'

And he began to push the pram on up the hillside, still talking to the baby, who seemed calm now and comfortable inside her green binding. By the time they reached the den, she was asleep. They put the pram by a big, shady rock and sat near it.

'Why did you wrap her in the leaves?' George asked.

After a while, Guido said: 'Nonna told me this, or I dream this. I don't know which!'

George looked at Guido. He was strange. He seemed to know so many peculiar, secret things. The question George couldn't answer was, could he trust him with *his* secret – the secret of Giovanni Capelli?

8

A Visit to 'Norridge'

In his lonely Clapham house and in his stuffy office at the Oceana Life Assurance Building, Robert Lewis sat and waited for the summer to pass.

Lots of horrible things were happening to Robert Lewis. First, he was getting constipation from all the hopeless frozen dinners he was eating. Second, the dog, Garibaldi, had decided to pine for George and did nothing but lie on its Happy Dreamer Doggybed all day and whimper. Third, the Boomerang Bonus Plan wasn't working too well any more. It had too many bad points, Robert's clients told him, like it was complicated and the money you saved took so long to boomerang back to you, you felt as if you might be dead before it actually did.

All in all, life for Robert Lewis had become difficult and lonely. After he'd found out what had happened to George, he'd planned to get straight on an aeroplane to Sicily. He'd been about to go and buy his ticket, when Serafima Smith had come round and said sternly to him: 'Don't do that, my friend! If you do that, Anna will never come back to you – *never!*'

Serafima Smith had been very bossy with him and told

him to sit down and listen and not interrupt. Then, she had begun to tell him things about Anna he had never really known until now, or if he *had* known them, he certainly hadn't bothered to understand them properly.

'What you're not twigging, Robert,' said Serafima, 'is this big question of family.'

'Of course I'm "twigging" it, Serafima,' Robert began. 'I've "twigged" that Anna cares so little about her family, she just runs off and leaves us.'

'No, no!' yelled Serafima. 'Not *your* family, *stupido*! The family of Violetta. The *famiglia* in Sicily!'

Robert sighed. He didn't feel like a lecture about how much Anna loved her family. 'I've taken Anna back to Aquilone every year I could afford it,' he said. But Serafima was shaking her head.

'I know, I know,' she said, 'but you still don't understand what family is for Anna. You remember when Vincente died, how she cried and cried?'

'I didn't know her then.'

'Well, she cried and cried. And now for Violetta.'

'Why for Violetta? Violetta's not dying.'

'She will die soon. She is very old. In this country, all your old people are by themselves. In little sad houses. Or in the Old People's Homes. But not in Sicily. In Sicily, old people are the *centre* of the family! Not sad. Not neglected. No! They drink with the family. They tell their stories and everyone listens to them. And they don't die alone. We are there. They die with the family.'

Robert nodded. He thought of his own father, on his own now in a little leaky house in Hampshire, getting meals from the Social Services three times a week. Suddenly, he felt sorry about this, sorry about neglecting the old man the way he did. He got up and poured Serafima and himself glasses of cheap Italian wine. Serafima took her glass and continued talking.

'You see, Robert, each year Anna's worrying more and more. She sees Violetta getting so old, her legs so bad. She tries to talk to you, to tell you she is still *part* of Violetta, still belonging in Sicily. But you don't listen.'

'I did, Serafima . . .'

'Well, you don't understand, then. You tell Anna, "I am your family now. You must forget your mother".'

'No. I didn't ever say this.'

'Yes, you do! And Anna is getting so unhappy. She knows you will not allow a long stay in Sicily. So she moves out into my house. She tells me, "I love Robert, Serafima, and I love George. But I have to go to Violetta".'

The cheap wine was rather revolting and bitter, but Robert took a big gulp of it before he said: 'Why did she take George away?'

'Because,' said Serafima, 'she wants him to *know* Violetta, before she dies.'

Robert was quiet. He'd been feeling very angry, but now he didn't really feel angry any more. Just confused. Should he go to Sicily, or should he wait? Would Anna come home? Would she send George back in time for the autumn term at school?

In the days that had followed Serafima's visit, he'd decided not to go to Sicily. Be patient, he told himself. But now the summer was passing. It was August already. The days were going by with nothing decided. And they were lonely days. Robert felt very melancholy with his constipation and his unhappy dog. Friends didn't visit him often. He felt old, even though he was only thirty-five.

Then, one morning, he decided to put poor old Garibaldi in his car and drive down to Hampshire to visit his father. He hoped that seeing this ancient father of his would make him feel young again.

Norman Reginald Lewis, nicknamed 'Norridge' by his family (a combination name: 'Nor' and 'Reg' joined together) was seventy-six and very rude to the world. He swore a great deal and called people 'rotters' and 'buggers' and 'nits'. When his wife, Constance, had been alive, he hadn't sworn quite so often, but now that he was alone in his dilapidated house, he swore all the time and shouted and stamped and even threw things at the dogs who peed on his lawn and sometimes at the Social Services people, who brought him Meals on Wheels. He was also very clumsy and broke things quite often, sometimes by mistake, sometimes on purpose, and even wounded himself on gadgets he'd never got the hang of, like tin-openers.

Norridge was very stubborn, too. Since Robert had been a child, Norridge had insisted on calling him 'Bertie', which Robert hated. Very many times, he'd asked Norridge not to call him Bertie any more, but Norridge paid no attention.

The day of Robert's visit to his father was sunny and fine. The lanes of Hampshire were green, and in Norridge's garden, his grass was a bit too long and green for his liking. He'd stuck one of Constance's old sunhats on his bald head and had gone out to see if he could start the lawnmower. But it wouldn't start. When Robert drove up, he saw his father swearing at it and kicking it.

'Silly bugger!' he was shouting. 'Idiotic invention!'

Robert and Garibaldi got out of the car. Norridge was actually very pleased to see his son, but you wouldn't have known this from the way he greeted him.

'So, you've turned up, have you, Bertie?' he said, giving the mower one last kick. 'P'raps you'll make yourself useful and get this ruddy nuisance thing going, eh?'

'I'll try, father,' said Robert.

It was a hot day and Robert had had a long drive and he didn't feel like mowing Norridge's lawn (on which Garibaldi was now peeing). But he took his jacket off and rolled up his sleeves and began to tug at the pull-starter. He pulled again and again, as hard as he could, but the machine wouldn't come to life.

'When did you last use the mower, father?' asked Robert.

'Dunno,' said Norridge. 'That nit from the bungalow usually does the lawn for me.'

'Why don't we leave it for him, then?'

'Not likely,' said Norridge. 'I want it going today. Look at this grass!'

Robert tried again. Nothing happened. He unscrewed the petrol cap and peered into the little tank. It was empty.

'No petrol, father,' he announced.

'What?' said Norridge. 'I told that nincompoop to fill it up. Can't trust a bloomin' soul these days. Everyone says "Yes" when they mean "No". Can't trust the government

any more. Can't trust NATO. Can't even trust the BBC. All liars, cheats and rotters!'

Norridge seemed to feel a bit better after this outburst and decided to invite Robert inside his house for a cool drink. Norridge had a passion for Lucozade. Some days, all he had to eat or drink was Lucozade. His few remaining teeth were starting to rot from all the Lucozade he drank, but he didn't care. He was old. His teeth would fall out anyway.

Robert didn't much like Lucozade, but he was thirsty, so he drank the glass Norridge poured for him and looked round the messy kitchen rather forlornly. It was really a dump, this kitchen of Norridge's. It was full of old milkbottles, burnt saucepans, mouldy tins, spilt cereal, and dirty dishes. It stank. Nothing ever seemed to be put away, or washed, or emptied, or tidied. The rubbish bin was overflowing. It was awful.

'Need a bit of a tidy up, father,' said Robert.

Norridge scratched his head through the flowery sunhat.

'That nit, Mrs Bradshaw, doesn't come to help out any more. Good riddance, I said. Always moaning, that woman!'

'Doesn't anyone come to help you?'

'Nope. Just let me stew in my own juice.'

'We must get you someone to help you in the house.'

'I'll manage on me own. Hate busybodies. All nits in this village. How's Anna, then, Bertie? She and George still in Sicily, are they?'

Robert looked down at his Lucozade glass. 'Yes, father.'

Norridge looked up sharply. He liked Anna. He liked the

wonderful meals she made and the way she hugged people very tightly. She made him wish, sometimes, that Constance was still alive to give him a hug. 'Left you, eh?' said Norridge.

Robert didn't reply.

'Eh, Bertie?' Norridge went on. 'Cleared off, has she? Done a bunk?'

'Yes,' said Robert. 'She says she wants to spend some time with her mother.'

'Does she?' said Norridge delightedly. 'Look after her mother, eh? Well, that's jolly good, if you ask me. Bet the mother deserves looking after more than you, eh, Bert?'

Robert shrugged.

'I think that's first class!' said Norridge. 'They know how to do things properly in proper families. And George will learn all that from them. Not like us. Too selfish. Terrible selfish lot, we are.'

'I don't think so,' said Robert.

'Oh? Think you're Jesus of Nazareth, what, Bertie?' And he slapped his knee and laughed.

'I always did my best for Anna,' Robert said.

'Did your best? Well, maybe. But was your "best" any good? Was it worth doing? That's the question to ask.'

'I worked. I supported her, I was a good husband . . .'

'Were you any *fun*, though, Bertie?'

'What?'

'I've never seen you be much fun. Not since you were ten. Miserable bugger, you are really.'

'If you're going to criticise me, father . . .'

'Criticise? Of course I'm going to criticise. Anna's left

you and Anna's a damn fine woman, so there must be something wrong with you. If we find out what it is, she might come back. It's your best bloody hope!'

Robert felt cross. He was beginning to wish he'd never come. He'd hoped to feel young and strong beside the seventy-six-year-old Norridge, but actually it was Norridge who seemed full of beans and Robert who felt old and sad.

After they'd drunk the Lucozade, Robert suggested that he take Norridge out to a pub for lunch and Norridge looked very pleased. The Meals on Wheels never came on a Saturday. All Norridge had in his larder was a bit of bacon and some corned beef. And he liked pubs. You could shout in a pub and no one told you off, you could even get a bit drunk if you wanted to.

So they put Garibaldi (who had cheered up a lot, now that he could smell the countryside) back into the car and drove to a pub called *The Sheepshearer* in a nearby village.

Here, Norridge suddenly decided that he was very hungry, and this is what he ate: four slices of cold lamb, three pickled onions, a jacket potato, cheese and biscuits and apple pie with custard. He also drank three pints of Guinness and his face became very red and shiny, and instead of being his usual rude self in the pub, he became very jolly and full of laughter.

Seeing him like this, Robert felt sad that no one cared for him any more, or cooked him good food, or talked to him.

When they got back from the pub, Norridge had a little sleep in his favourite armchair, and Robert put on an old apron that had belonged to Constance, his mother, and set about tidying and cleaning Norridge's kitchen.

He noticed, while he was doing this, how many things were broken or faulty in Norridge's house – panes of glass missing from the kitchen windows, big damp patches on the ceiling, taps and sink all old and rusty, no shade on the lightbulb, no clean towels anywhere and all the cupboards scuffed or damaged.

It used to be a clean, pretty house. How had it become like this? It had been neglected, that's all. It wasn't hard to neglect things and just not notice when they stayed broken or dirty or damaged. It wasn't hard to neglect people, either, especially if they were rude and awkward, like Norridge. You just forgot about them. You said to yourself, 'oh, he's all right'. But Norridge wasn't all right. He ate poor food. His house had become a slum.

When Norridge woke up from his sleep, Robert had finished cleaning the kitchen and he had brought his father a cup of tea. The old man still had his bright colour, and he felt very refreshed, he said, after his nap.

They talked about George for a while and about how much Robert missed his son. Then Robert said to Norridge: 'I had an idea while you were asleep. Why don't I come and stay with you for a while? Get everything mended in the house again. Get the garden tidy. Get you all shipshape again?'

Norridge looked disbelievingly at his son. 'You don't have to stay here, Bertie-boy. Too much of a mess here.'

'No,' said Robert, 'I don't have to, but I'd *like* to come. For me as well as for you. I'd like a break from London. I've just sat and felt sorry for myself there, that's all I've done.'

'What about that old Boomerang job?'

'It's all right. A bit dull.'

'Rotters might give you the sack, if you don't turn up.'

'No, they won't. I'll take a holiday. It's summer. I'm owed some holiday time.'

'Well, I dunno, Bert. I dunno . . .'

But Norridge *did* know. He was very happy that Robert was going to stay. Now, he could send those nits from the Social Services away, the lawn would be cut and he'd have company at last. He wasn't going to say this to old Bertie, but he hadn't felt so pleased about anything in a long, long time.

9

The Storm

'You know what is a tanning factory?' Guido asked George, one evening at the den.

'No,' said George.

'A tanning factory is a very important place. Where the leather dies.'

'*What?*' said George.

'Where the leather died.'

'You mean, where they dye leather?'

'Yes. Very important.'

'So?'

'This is where I begin my business career. In a very important tanning factory in New York, West Side.'

'When?' asked George.

'In two years. Signor Albertini promises me. It's very good, no?'

'Yes,' said George half-heartedly. He didn't think a tanning factory sounded like a very good place to work in: dyeing animal skins different colours sounded awful. George said again, 'Why don't you stay here, Guido?' and again Guido said, 'This place is no good.' And again George wondered what he really meant. Was it only that no one in

Aquilone, except Mario Albertini, was rich? Probably, it was. This was what Guido wanted – to be rich, like his godfather – and it certainly seemed difficult for anyone to get rich in Aquilone.

When the boys arrived for supper at Sofia's house, they found Enzo in a very bad mood, pacing about on the terrace and staring up at the sky.

'Stormy's come,' he explained to George, 'but come too late! He will hurt my *olivi*.'

George knew how precious Enzo's olive crop was. The money he got from this kept the family going for several months. Without this money, life would become very hard for them. Sofia and Anna and Guido and Violetta knew this, so everyone was quiet and anxious that evening, hoping the treacherous little wind that had got up would die down by morning, hoping the storm wouldn't come.

But in the night, the storm began. The wind sang down the chimneys and in through the cracks in the stone walls and all the shutters on Violetta's small house banged and rattled, and then the rain came driving in drenching gusts and thunder echoed round the mountain.

George lay in his narrow bed and listened, and felt afraid. The lightning was white at his window, making the room flicker in ghostly light. He thought of the ghost he had seen and shivered and pulled his covers round his head. What was going to happen to him and to the family? Had the Capelli ghost brought this terrible storm? What would become of them all, if the olives were destroyed?

There was movement in the house. Someone tip-toed to George's door and knocked softly. It was Anna. She was carrying a candle. The storm had knocked out the electricity supply. Anna's face was a strange, yellowy colour above the little candle flame. She sat down by George's bed and stroked his hair. 'Can't you sleep, Giorgio?'

'No. What's going to happen about the olives, Mamma?'

'I don't know. Perhaps this storm passes quickly.'

'But what if it doesn't?'

'Then we will all help to save what we can. Now, try to sleep. Tomorrow, we will all be working.'

She was about to go, but George sat up in his bed and called her back. 'I want to tell you something, Mamma.'

'It's so late. Go to sleep.'

'No. I have to tell you now.'

She sat on his bed. The thunder seemed to be moving away a little, moving north beyond the volcano rim.

'I saw a ghost . . .' said George. He found he was shivering. He held on to the sleeve of Anna's dressing gown.

'Don't be stupid,' said Anna, but her eyes had darted to his face and they were full of alarm.

'I *did*,' said George.

'Where? Where you see any silly ghost?'

'There was this long driveway. There were trees on both sides. I saw it there. It was Giovanni Capelli.'

Anna looked petrified. She pressed her hand on George's mouth. 'Don't say things like this!'

George tugged Anna's hand away. 'I *did*, Mamma. I saw the man in the shrine photograph.'

'No, no, no . . .'

'It was him. He smiled at me. Then he vanished.'

'It was someone else.'

93

'No. It was that man who died – Giovanni Capelli.'

'Where you see him? Where? When?'

'A few days ago. In this driveway. I told you. Where there are two lines of tall cedars.'

'The Capelli House,' she said gravely, 'that was the Capelli House.'

'Who lives there now, Mamma?'

Anna held George's shoulders tightly now and put her face near to his. 'There are no ghosts in Sicily,' she said, 'you imagine this man, that's all.'

'I didn't imagine him. Tell me who lives in that house, Mamma.'

'No one. And you didn't see no one, okay?'

'I did, though. He walked towards me . . .'

'Don't think of this anymore, Giorgio.'

'I can't help it, Mamma.'

Anna hugged George. 'You are safe here,' she said. 'This is my village, my house, where I grew up. This is my precious place I wanted you to know, before you grow up and make your life in England, before Nonna leaves us . . .'

The candle flickered. George pressed his nose into Anna's shoulder and whispered in a small, frightened voice. 'Is Nonna going to die?'

There was a moment's pause. George sensed Anna's hesitation before she said calmly: 'One day, maybe quite soon, she will.'

George couldn't speak. The terrible ghost, the storm, the thought of losing Nonna; he was filled with the fear and sadness of these things and all he could do was hold on to his mother tightly, and they sat like this together for a long time, Anna rocking George gently, like when he was a tiny child.

When, eventually, she went back to her room, she left the candle burning by his bed. With this little light by him, George tried to sleep, but all night he kept thinking he saw ghosts in his room. And all night, the storm turned in circles above Aquilone, and the rain and the wind tore into the silvery olive branches and knocked the olives to the ground like a hail of stones.

By morning, the centre of the storm had moved far inland, but following it came a soft, blanketing rain, and all the hillsides were shrouded in mist.

Though no one in the family had had much sleep, Sofia and Violetta woke them early. The olives that had fallen would rot if they were left on the ground in the rain; they had to be gathered.

Everyone was given baskets, slung round their necks on leather straps, and then they set out in a little tired line for the olive pastures. Violetta, who was too old to do this hard, stooping work, took Filomena into her house and rocked her to sleep, and made a big pot of soup, ready for midday.

Then the work of the olive gathering began. The ground was covered with the green fruit. It was almost impossible not to step on the olives and crush them as you worked, scooping them up with wet, cold fingers and throwing them into the heavy baskets. It was monotonous, back-breaking work: so many fallen olives, so few people. The rain soaked your hair and ran down your neck. In no time at all, your clothes were wet through, and still the rain went on falling,

and still the carpet of olives stretched on and on.

Enzo's rusty tractor was driven up to the corner of the first pasture. Attached to it was an old wooden hopper, into which the full basketloads were poured. When the hopper was full, Enzo drove this to his barn. Here, the olives would be washed and loaded up for collection by the big olive oil company in Catania. From this company would come the payments on which Enzo depended.

They worked until late afternoon, only stopping to devour Violetta's good soup and three loaves of bread. No one complained. Even Alfredo and Anna-Maria toiled on, filling up basket after basket, their hands and faces and knees smudged with the dark olive stain.

By four o'clock, three hopper-loads had been taken to the barn and Enzo had cheered up. And now, in the wake of the blanketing rain, a sudden brilliant blue sky appeared and the hot sun made the damp ground steam. Enzo stood up and stretched and looked up at the new blue sky. 'Okay!' he shouted. 'Stoppy stoppy! Everyone. Everyone get their knickers! We go to the *sea*!'

Six faces stared at Enzo in amazement. The sea! It was quite a long way to the sea. Usually, Enzo grumbled and moaned if he had to drive them there. But today was different. The family had worked on the olives since six that morning. Only a sprinkling of the precious crop remained to be gathered. Disaster had approached, but Enzo's army of workers had fended it off. The sea was their reward. Guido gave a whoop of joy, and Alfredo and Anna-Maria began to jump about in excited circles.

Violetta said she would keep Filomena with her. She

stood with the baby and waved as the family piled into the Chevvy, which sagged under the weight of so many people and coughed and wheezed a few times before it would start. Then it lurched off down the curving road and sped towards the distant, beckoning water.

Though it was very blue, the sea was cold and choppy and full of seaweed and debris. After storms, it was often rather troubled, Anna told George, as if all its secrets had been stirred up.

The beach was rocky and pebbly. The stones hurt your feet as you waded out. But once you were swimming, it was fine. George was a strong swimmer and he and Guido swam out to a tiny island of rock, covered with mussels and barnacles. From here, you could see right down the coast and high above it, to where the last storm clouds sat above Etna. It's beautiful, George decided. With its cypresses and olives and mimosa, with its stone houses and its new white-washed villas, it was a fabulous place – his place, his mother's island. Perhaps he would never leave it now? Perhaps he would go to Guido's school and become a real Sicilian boy? He sat on the barnacled rock and thought about these things and stared till his eyes ached at the great vista of the volcano and all its green hillsides, which seemed to come pouring out of the dark clouds and arrange themselves along the seashore just for his benefit.

Then, in among the black bulk of cloud that sat on the mountain, George's eye suddenly caught a tiny flash of red.

'Guido!' he called. 'Look!'

He pointed upwards. Guido, who was swimming near the

rock, trod water and stared up. After a few seconds, it came again, a flash of fiery red like crimson lightning, there for the briefest moment, then gone. George looked at Guido and saw on his cousin's face a look of terror, such as he'd never seen in his life.

'*Gesú!*' gasped Guido, and by mistake swallowed water and began to choke. He coughed and coughed, struggled to the rock and held on to it, gasping. George made as if to help him up, but Guido shook his head. 'No, no!' he said, and pulled George back into the water. 'Swim!' he yelled. 'Swim fast!'

George obeyed. As they swam, their eyes stayed fixed on the volcano. The black cloud sat tight on its rim. Then, up through the black cloud and spurting high into the clear sky above it came a gush of flame, higher than any fountain, brighter than any firework, a flame thrown up from the belly of the earth, from its brimstone centre.

She's going!' cried Guido. '*Il vulcano! Il vulcano!*'

They swam on. The sun was still bright on the water, but at his back now George could feel a sudden wind start to swell the sea and strong waves began to push at them. All along the beach, they saw the trees shiver and sway. And the moving of the trees alerted Enzo and Sofia and Anna, and the grownups looked about them to see where this sudden wind had come from.

Then Enzo looked up. What Enzo saw and what Guido and George saw, as they struggled forward on the buffeting waves, was an explosion so colossal, so fearful and devouring that the whole of one side of the mountain seemed to be thrust in a million fragments out into the void, where it appeared to be suspended for a second before it fell and the hills beneath disappeared in smoke and dust and falling rock. And out of the crater rim, the bubbling burning blood of the earth began to pour and over all the fallen rocks and stones, rivers of fire began to flow.

The noise of the explosion was deafening, as if the world was splitting. Then the sound was overtaken by the screams of Anna and Sofia and the children, who came running to their parents and hid their faces in Sofia's wide belly.

Guido and George could see Enzo yelling to them now to hurry. They battled on, grim in their struggle with the sea and with their fear. Only Guido knew that far beneath their feet, the water could be sliding and slipping back, to be sucked up by the wind into a wave so vast that when it broke on the beach, it would destroy not only the people stranded there, but all the trees and all the houses and cafés and shops, pounding them to fragments and splinters, as if they'd never existed.

And then, at the same moment, Guido and George remembered Violetta. Nonna Violetta! She was high up on that hill, so near to where the side of the mountain had fallen! She was alone with little Filomena. She couldn't run. She couldn't go running away from the falling stones and the rivers of fire. Someone had to reach her, before it was too late. But who? Here, they were miles from her. Who, of their neighbours in Aquilone, would remember her? Would all the families just gather up their possessions and run away, abandoning her? 'Nonna! Nonna!' Guido was repeating and repeating as he swam on. He saw his father gather up both the smaller children in his wide arms and run with them to where the Chevvy was parked.

Sofia and Anna were waving towels frantically and calling: 'Guido! Giorgio!' Dizzy and choked from the effort of their swim, the two boys tottered on to the hurting shingle. Anna and Sofia thrust the towels round them and the four of them ran to Enzo who had the Chevvy engine started. The few other families who had also been on the beach were running to their cars. They, too, knew about the giant wave that might come. Some of the women were crying and wailing. For here was the disaster they prayed each night of their lives would never happen. It *had* happened. They fled from the beach. They fled back to villages they knew might be in the path of the lava. Nowhere was safe. They drove, like Enzo, fast, racing back to save their homes, save their animals, save anything they could. 'Save Violetta,' George prayed. 'Please God, please, please save Violetta.'

The Chevvy turned off the coast road and began to climb towards Aquilone. George and Guido struggled into their clothes. The sun went in and a horrible dark spread across the landscape. Fear was racing in all their hearts, fear for everyone and everything they loved, fear for what seemed like the end of the world.

10

Into Darkness

Up and up the hillside the Chevvy climbed. Its gears ground at each steep turn of the road and Enzo swore at it. Was it, after all, going to be his coffin in a way he hadn't imagined? Suddenly, he hated the car. What use are possessions, he thought, if Violetta and Filomena are dead, if all the olive trees are burned?

The black cloud of smoke pouring from the volcano had quite obscured the sun and it was getting darker and darker. Sofia held the two little children tightly to her. Both of them were whimpering with fear. Anna put her arm round George and Guido, who sat close together, each glad of the other's presence. In Sicily, boys Guido's age were meant to be sensible and strong and help protect the younger children. But Guido didn't know whether he could be strong now. He thought he might succeed if George was strong, too.

They heard the siren of a fire engine behind them on the narrow road and pulled over to let it pass. 'One fire engine!' said Anna, 'and the whole mountain is burning!'

They were almost at Monte Passerino now. The lava flow was still way above them. Monte Passerino seemed quite safe. Would Aquilone be safe? Would Violetta be safe? The car lurched on. It sounded sick. The engine noise had a peculiar rattle and thump in it, and when Enzo tried to accelerate, it whirred and whined. Enzo banged the steering wheel and screamed at the car: '*Stupida machina!*' It was slowing down. Enzo was pressing the accelerator pedal, but the Chevvy was going slower and slower. It rolled a few yards and then stuttered to a·halt. '*Imbecille!*' Enzo yelled.

He got out and Guido got out and they lifted up the heavy old bonnet and stared at the engine, which was boiling hot and smoking. The fan belt had broken. Enzo tugged it out and waved it in the air like a snake he was about to kill. Without a new belt, the car wouldn't go. Enzo hurled the broken belt away from him and stared at his family, huddled in the car. How small and frail they looked! If one tiny hurled rock could kill the giant, Goliath, what chance did ordinary people stand when a mountain fell?

They were still a long way from Aquilone, but it seemed relatively safe here, far from the rockfall and the lava streams. Enzo told Sofia and Anna to stay with Alfredo and Anna-Maria in the car, but neither would listen to him. They had to get to Aquilone. They had to know what had happened to Violetta and Filomena. Enzo protested that it was too far for the little children to walk, but Sofia replied that they would carry them. She wasn't going to be left in the middle of nowhere. She was going on up. So they set off, the same little line of people who, at dawn that very day, had set off for the olive groves.

Monte Passerino – deserted when George had gone there with his letter – was full of people. A slight earth tremor had been felt here. Cracks had appeared in some of the buildings. People were loading their possessions into cars and onto carts and barrows. The place wasn't safe, they said. The buildings could fall. Another earthquake could follow. And Aquilone? asked Enzo and Sofia. Was Aquilone safe? Had buildings fallen there? Yes, they were told, buildings had fallen. Rescue workers had gone up. And above Aquilone? Were the houses safe there? The people of Monte Passerino shook their heads sadly. They'd heard some big rocks had fallen. Above Aquilone, there would be many dead . . .

They pushed on then, through the throng of people, past furniture standing in the street and boxes of bed linen and copper cooking pots. One old man was sitting on a stool at an upright piano that was standing on the pavement. His face was blank with confusion, as if no one had told him what had happened or why the houses were cracking or why all his belongings were being loaded onto a cart.

Outside Monte Passerino, on the road that was getting very dark as the vast pall of smoke covered the sky, they met the first people coming down from Aquilone. All were people they knew. Many of them were crying and white with shock. They stopped and embraced Enzo and Sofia, who asked them, 'Did anyone go up for Violetta?' They shrugged and gestured. They didn't know, they said. 'No time . . .' they mumbled.

Another fire engine passed them. Above them, in the near darkness, they could see the lava cascading down in its fiery streams. It was strangely, horribly beautiful. The wind sighed and whistled. How lonely it seemed suddenly, on this road they knew so well! And frightening. Frightening to be trudging on in darkness, not knowing what they would find. As they passed the Capelli house, George looked away from it. He was trying to hold himself tall and straight, as he saw Guido was doing.

Alfredo and Anna-Maria were so tired now, they didn't have the strength to cry any more. Alfredo was carried on Enzo's shoulders, Anna-Maria on Sofia's. They clung tightly to their parents heads as, step by step, their village came nearer. They longed to sleep, and then to wake up and be told it was all a dream. But it was real: the creeping darkness, the wind at their backs, the terrible fire above them and then, as they came to the village itself, the familiar houses still standing, but most of them abandoned, silent, ghostly. It was worse than any dream they'd ever dreamed.

The track to their own house lay behind the church. Now they saw that one of the twin towers of the Aquilone church had cracked and part of it had fallen. Their path was strewn with rubble. The grownups crossed themselves and prayed as they picked their way past it. If the church itself could fall, then God must really be angry . . .

They heard a car coming towards them. Enzo stepped out to warn the driver about the rubble on the path. The headlights dazzled him. The car slowed. It was a wide car. As Enzo went up to it, they all saw that it was Mario Albertini's Cadillac and Mario Albertini was at the wheel.

'Signor Albertini!' Enzo yelled, 'the road's blocked down there behind the church. You won't get through.'

To the surprise of everyone, Mario Albertini jumped out of his car and went to Enzo, who was still carrying Alfredo,

and threw his long arms round him and burst into tears. The family watched and stared. No one could ever remember seeing Mario Albertini cry. 'Enzo, Enzo,' he said, 'what sorrow for this village! What heartbreak!' Then, he pulled away and went to the Cadillac. He opened the back door of the car and lifted out a large bundle, wrapped in a blanket, and put it gently into Enzo's arms. It was Filomena. Enzo held the baby to him. The family crowded round and Sofia began to scream, thinking her baby was dead. But Enzo could feel the warmth of the child. He kissed Filomena and saw her open her eyes. She was alive. 'She's alive, Sofia,' said Mario Albertini, 'and she is not harmed. I saved her.'

It seemed that everyone was crying then. Even Guido, who wanted to show that he was strong, felt choked as Mario Albertini related what had happened. George couldn't understand what he was saying, so Anna whispered bits of what he said in English and Mario Albertini's story came to George in strange disconnected sentences: '. . . he was walking. He saw the mountain go. He was about to run back to his house. He saw the pram. Stones from the rockfall were tumbling near it. Pram all alone. No one with it. He began to run up. He reached it. He called and called. No one. Bigs rocks crashing. Houses gone above. So he ran down . . .'

Mario Albertini stopped speaking and Anna stopped speaking and there was silence on the road, except for the sighing of the wind. The family looked at the man who had, by an act of bravery, saved Filomena and felt a gratitude they would never be able to express. In the same moment, everyone understood the one thing he hadn't been able to say: Violetta was dead. They stood in a huddle. Helpless. Grieving. They felt empty of words.

It was night now. They lay out on mattresses in a meadow just below the olive pastures. It was cold and there were no stars in the sky.

Scores of firemen and ambulancemen had made their way up to the line of the rockfall and were trying, with earth-movers and drills and axes, to sift through the huge pieces of rubble that had buried Violetta's house and many houses further up. The little corner of grass, where Filomena's pram had been snatched to safety, was no more than twenty yards from where Violetta lay buried. The route up the mountain that Anna had followed as a girl no longer existed.

From time to time, Anna or Sofia or Enzo would get up and climb wearily to where the rescue people worked, and stand staring at the place where Violetta's house had been. The body would be deep, deep down, the firemen told them. It could be hours before they could reach it. So they would stand and stare for a while longer, with hunched shoulders, and remember little useless things about Violetta, like where she had planted her sunflowers, and the worn spot on her verandah where she always placed her chair. And then they would return to the field, and heat coffee on a camping stove they'd set up and try to get warm. They remembered too, to say a prayer of thanks that Filomena had been saved, that the lava streams had taken another course and wouldn't touch Aquilone, that their house was standing, that the olive trees were safe.

Guido and George had put their mattresses close together, some way from the grownups, and they talked quietly, huddled up in their grey blankets. The den was gone, they knew. They wondered if Fabio had been safe in his father's garage, or up there among the white rocks. They talked about Fabio, who would never move from Aquilone. Then, they talked about Mario Albertini and his saving of Filomena, and George now felt very confused about this man. Was he a murderer? Were the stories true about him killing Giovanni Capelli? Was he a good man, or was he a man capable of both acts of cruelty *and* acts of goodness? Was it right to hate him the way he did? On impulse, he decided to tell Guido that night about the Capelli ghost. He thought Guido would be amazed and shocked, but the boy only shrugged and said: 'The dead are very sad in Sicily.'

'Sad?' asked George. 'What do you mean?'

'Lonely,' said Guido, 'they are missing their families.'

'So you mean they try to come back, to visit their houses and everything?'

'Yes.'

'But the Capellis don't live in that house any more. It's deserted.'

'Yes. But the dead cannot know that.'

'You mean, they keep looking in all the old places?'

'Yes. Of course. I think Giovanni Capelli thinks you are his son. But then, he sees you are not, and he disappears.'

'He smiled at me.'

'Yes.'

'But I don't really believe that dead people come back, Guido.'

'You saw him.'

'I thought I did . . .'

'No. You did. In Sicily, they come back, these sad dead. Nonna will come back. You will see.'

'Nonna? I don't want Nonna to come back!'

'Well, you don't want. But she will. She will be lonely without Mamma and Anna. And without us, Giorgio.'

'I hope she doesn't.'

'I hope she does.'

But it was too sad, really, to talk about Nonna Violetta and the boys were suddenly silent. It had been a long and terrible day and eventually they fell into an exhausted, dream-filled sleep.

They were woken early. When they opened their eyes and looked at the field and at the sleeping family, they thought that snow had fallen. The grass and the stones and all the people rolled up in their grey blankets were covered with white dust. It had fallen on their own faces, too. They rubbed their eyes, stared at their hands. It was ash. A great cloud of ash had been sucked up into the sky, and now it had fallen, covering all the hills and trees and houses for miles around with a fine white powder the colour of bone.

People began talking in the field. One of the firemen, his uniform muddy and his face very tired, was talking to Anna and Sofia. The women then followed this man up the hill and Enzo came over to George and Guido.

'They find Nonna,' he said in English, laying his wide hands on the boys' heads. He looked very sad, but then he tugged the boys towards him roughly and said with a smile: 'Nonna make a bloody racket in the angel choir, eh?'

In the light of day, Enzo was able to examine the house for cracks and movement. It seemed quite sound. One chimney pot had fallen, but otherwise it was undamaged.

And it was inside the house that, later that morning, Violetta's body was laid on Enzo and Sofia's bed and covered by a clean sheet. The boys were sent off into the village to find Signor Cannone, the coffin-maker, but Signor Cannone's house had been badly damaged and he and his family were nowhere to be found. So it was Enzo who, with the help of George and Guido, lugged planks of pine from the timber yard and chiselled and planed the wood to make a coffin for Violetta. The women washed the mud and dust from Violetta's face and dressed her in her best black clothes, and then she was laid gently in the home-made coffin, and candles were lit all around her and a sweet incense was burned.

When George went into the strange, candlelit room, he found that he didn't feel like crying. Later, I'll probably cry, he thought. Instead, he found himself thinking about his life in London and wanting, more than anything else in the world, to be back there. So much had happened in Sicily since his arrival – so many things he didn't really understand. He felt more tired and confused than he'd ever felt in his life.

He pictured himself sitting at the desk in his London bedroom, not working, nor even reading or watching television, but just sitting in this reassuring and familiar place and staring at the wall.

11

The Way Back

News of the eruption of Mount Etna travelled all over the world very quickly. Helicopters flew in and took photographs of the lava streams and of the massive rockfall that had buried more than thirty houses. These photographs appeared on the television news in England the following day and were seen by Norridge, who was sitting in his favourite chair, drinking a Guinness.

'Good gracious!' Norridge said aloud, and then he began calling to Robert, who was loading their supper things into the new dishwasher he'd installed in Norridge's kitchen.

'Bertie!' he shouted. 'Trouble and strife, Bert!'

Robert appeared at the door. Norridge pointed to the TV screen. An English reporter was describing the scene in the villages below the volcano. 'People here,' he was saying, 'are taking no chances. They know that even if they're safe from the red-hot lava, earth tremors can be a devastating side-effect of volcanic activity. Indeed, they have already experienced one such tremor and many of the buildings have cracked or subsided. Most of the families I spoke to were leaving their homes . . .'

Robert stared at the TV in disbelief, his mouth open. 'Oh my God,' he said.

Norridge put down his Guinness and turned to his son.

'Better get to them, Bertie,' he said, 'better get on a plane double quick sharp!'

Robert was shaking his head, still not really believing what he was seeing. 'Anna . . .' he mumbled, 'George . . .'

Norridge got up decisively. 'You can't delay, old nit. You've got to get them home.'

Just then, the telephone rang. Robert hurried to answer it, fearing some terrible news. It was Serafima Smith.

'Robert,' she said urgently, 'you see the news?'

'Yes,' said Robert, 'I must get to them, Serafima . . .'

'Okay,' said Serafima, trying to sound as calm as she could, 'you and I will go tomorrow. There is one flight to Catania from Heathrow at five. I will book the tickets now. I will meet you at the airport at four. Okay?'

'Yes,' said Robert, 'I'll be there. Thank you, Serafima.'

He stood still. He was glad Serafima had taken charge. Tomorrow – if they were still alive – he would be with his wife and son.

Norridge came out of the sitting room and looked worriedly at Robert. 'Come on, Bert,' he said, 'don't fret like a twerp. You'll be there in a flash. Have a dose of Guinness.'

At ten past five the following day, a plane bound for Sicily was carrying Robert Lewis and Serafima Smith into the blue summer sky. As it climbed higher and higher, Robert remembered how Anna had sat, on a plane just like this one, and cried for the family she was leaving. He had felt cross, very cross and irritated that Anna could love people other than himself so much. But he knew better now. He knew that Anna had a right to love her family and her country, and that it was quite a *good* thing to spend time with your parents – as he had recently discovered by spending time with Norridge. He'd got to know the old man again, almost as well as when he was a boy. He was difficult and stubborn as a bad-tempered ox, but he could still be fun, he could still enjoy himself when he wasn't lonely, and he had courage. They'd begun to like each other again. And Robert felt ashamed of all the years he'd neglected Norridge. How could he have done this? Easy, really. He'd been selfish. The trouble with selfishness was that, in the end, you lost all the people who were close to you. Either they left you (like Anna), or you abandoned them (like Norridge). If this went on and on, you'd wind up completely alone. And this seemed a bit silly, when you remembered how many millions of people there were in the world.

It was quite a long flight to Catania, but Robert and Serafima hardly talked at all. Serafima thought not only about Anna, her friend, but about her own family in Messina. She decided that if all was well with Anna, she would go on to Messina and visit them. Like Anna's family, they were poor. She would buy her mother presents: dress material, kitchenware, some new dinner plates . . .

They were given a little meal on plastic trays, but neither Serafima nor Robert felt hungry. They sipped coffee. They saw the sun go down, and the evening begin to come on. They wondered what terrible things waited for them. They grew nervous. They looked at their watches. Half an hour

more . . . Then, the plane was turning. Ten minutes more .
. . It was turning and turning and beginning to descend
towards Catania airport.

No one waited for them. No one knew they were coming.
An old taxi would take them – if the road was passable – into
the darkness, towards Aquilone . . .

In the room where Violetta's body lay, the candles dripped
and dripped. The sweet incense smell seemed to be every-
where – in the folds of the curtains, in the creases of
people's clothes.

At suppertime, the priest had come. He'd held his ornate
sash against Violetta's white forehead and said some Latin
prayers.

It's all so peculiar, thought George. The flickering light,
the sugary smell, and everyone standing around, not saying
anything, just staying awake for Nonna. Death is peculiar,
he decided. People know so many millions of impossible-
seeming things, like how to split atoms, how to get astro-
nauts to the moon, but they hardly know anything about
death. They don't even know if God exists. Or Heaven. Or
ghosts, for that matter. Nobody knows for certain, beyond
all possible doubt. Not even Guido with his tales of the sad
dead. Not even the priest. Only Nonna knows, now. Either
she *is* something, somewhere, or she's nothing. But if you
don't exist any more, then you can't *know* that you don't
exist. You just end. You are darkness, nothingness. You are
eternity. George sighed. Death was the most peculiar thing
of all.

In this same way – with the candles and the body and the

incense – this family had stayed awake the night before Nonno Vincente was buried. The younger children were put to bed – in their own beds tonight, not on the mattresses in the field – but Guido and George were expected to stay with the grownups, to stay with Nonna till morning came and they buried her in the cemetery.

Sofia had banked up her stove and made a batch of little fruity buns. When it grew late, George and Guido started to yawn and they were told to eat the buns. Sweet wine was passed around, too, and they sipped at this, but they were so tired, they kept closing their eyes and drifting away into strange dreams.

It was hot and stuffy in the room. Anna looked round at her sister, watching her struggle, too, with tiredness. She wanted to cry for her mother, but oddly, the tears wouldn't come. She'd known, after all, that Violetta was going to die. It was this knowledge that had brought her back to Sicily. And now, what should she do? It seemed to Anna that with the death of her mother she'd loved so much, part of her life was over. The part she'd loved best, in a kind of way, the part when she was a little girl and running like a wild thing on these hills. Now, even Violetta's house had gone and her terrace and all her familiar, time-worn furniture. Even the goats and the goat pastures were buried and the way up the mountain would never be the same. All these things would just become memories. They wouldn't exist ever again.

Anna sipped the sweet wine and stared at Violetta's coffin. Her thoughts were disturbed by an unexpected sound in the room and Anna looked round to see what it was. Enzo was snoring! Anna looked across at Sofia and Sofia looked at

Enzo and smiled. 'Let him sleep,' she whispered.

And Guido and George were sleeping, too, lolling against each other. They'd tried and tried to keep awake, but they couldn't; they were too exhausted. So Violetta's two daughters, Anna and Sofia, kept the wake for their mother until, soon after midnight, they heard the sound of a car and Sofia got up and tiptoed to the door.

Anna listened. The car stopped. She heard voices. Some English words, some Italian. One was a man's voice and she wondered if Mario Albertini had come. They seemed to be talking for a long time before Sofia came back quietly into the room, looked at Anna solemnly and said: '*E Roberto, Anna.*'

Anna sat stock still for a moment, and then with a movement that seemed to her to be as swift as flight, she ran from the room and into the kitchen and threw herself into Robert's arms, and started to cry and cry. He held her tightly and just repeated her name over and over, 'Anna . . . Anna . . . Anna . . .'

Serafima Smith sat down on one of the hard kitchen chairs and blew her nose.

George opened his eyes and stared up at Sofia, who was prodding him awake. He felt confused. It was meant to be night-time. He knew he was meant to be keeping awake for Nonna. But the light in the room was different: it was early morning. He looked at the candles and saw that most of them had gone out.

'I'm sorry, Sofia,' he mumbled. 'I went to sleep.'

'Come,' said Sofia.

'What?' said George.

'Come with me.'

George rubbed his eyes and got up. Only Guido, he now saw, was left in the room with Violetta. He was fast asleep, too.

He followed Sofia. He could smell coffee simmering. He could hear voices in the kitchen. He went in. Sitting at the table, drinking coffee, were Enzo, Anna-Maria, Alfredo, Anna, Serafima Smith and his father! His father got up and crossed the room towards him. He looked thin, George noticed, but rather brown from the sun. He wasn't wearing the suit he usually wore, but a bright pink shirt and a silk scarf round his neck.

'Dad!' said George, 'you got my letter?'

Robert smiled and shook his head. 'No. I didn't get a letter. I just decided to come here.'

He gave George a hug then. George looked over his father's shoulder at his mother and he saw that she was smiling. So he smiled too, and in that instant, he knew that very soon they would all be going home to England.

They buried Violetta that morning. Enzo lent Robert a frayed black jacket (far too big for him) to cover up his pink shirt. At the graveside, Robert stood next to Anna, holding her hand.

Not many people came from the village. Above it, rescue work was still going on and many of the people were too frightened to return to their houses. The volcano was quiet now, however, and the sky above the Aquilone cemetery was very blue that morning of Violetta's burial. Gradually,

over the weeks to come, the life of the village would return to what it had been. The church tower would be mended. The villagers would come back and repair the cracks in their walls and make shrines for their dead, and pray that no more tragedies would happen in their lifetimes.

Mario Albertini came to the funeral. George couldn't help still disliking this man and thinking, meanly, that his big black car was just right for a funeral and imagining it arriving, silently, at the funeral of poor Giovanni Capelli.

But George knew that Guido and Sofia and even Enzo thought of this rich man as their protector and benefactor. He was their link with worlds they didn't really understand – with America, with money and fast cars and luxury, with success. And it wasn't hard to imagine Guido going off to America, starting work in the tanning factory, working hard and doing well, growing up in New York, wearing flashy clothes. And then one day, becoming someone important, a kind of benefactor in his turn.

George knew that his own route to being grown up was different, very different. It wouldn't start in a factory. It would start with school work and exams. His way into the grown-up world would be through knowledge – knowledge of all kinds of thousands of things – and part of that knowledge had begun right here, in Aquilone. I don't want to lose the Aquilone bit of me, George thought. I want to come here very often.

But summer was passing now. George couldn't help feeling excited about the thought of returning to school, seeing Gishy and even Beamish and Fenbow (those idiots!) and riding his bike again and playing pop music and being in the school Christmas Show and taking Garibaldi for walks on Clapham Common. So different, this life was, so far-away-seeming, that when they all returned from the cemetery, George decided to go off to Guido's room and be by himself for a while, just to think about this other life and remember what it was going to be like.

He sat down on Guido's bed and looked at the white-washed walls and the little ivory Jesus they'd nailed up there to watch over him. It was an almost identical room to the one he'd slept in in Violetta's house, the room now smashed and buried by the fallen rock. One day, quite soon, Guido would leave this room and go to America. But now it was George who was saying goodbye.

'I'm leaving Aquilone,' he whispered. 'I've got to. But I will come back. I'm part of you, Aquilone.'

He stared at the wooden bed, where he'd lain on the first night of his illness and then at the big old wardrobe where Guido's faded clothes were hanging. Then, a tiny sound made him look down and he saw, in the dark space at the foot of the wardrobe, a small brown fieldmouse poking its nose into the room. George stared and stared at it. 'Nonna,' he whispered, hardly daring to breathe, 'it's Nonna.'

And he heard her voice then, very tiny, very far away, but talking in English very fast, as if she could only stay for the shortest time and yet had many words to say.

'So much . . .' said the tiny voice, 'so much to do, Gior-gio. So much to do and only one little life to do it in. Busy! So busy, Nonna is. Busy as a mouse. For the world is busy, you see? And so huge, my chicken, so huge!'

*

At twelve o'clock on the morning of September 1st, Norridge put on a clean shirt and tie and attempted to comb into place his wild, untidy white hair.

'That's better!' he said to his reflection in the mirror. 'That's more the biscuit!'

He then went to his front door (which Robert had painted a new shade of dark green) and hung up a piece of cardboard, on which he had written in large black letters the word WELCOME.

He stood back and looked at it. He felt quite proud of it and really rather happy altogether. Robert and Anna and George had been back in their London home for a week now and today, Saturday, they were coming down to see him and to collect Garibaldi.

It was a fine morning, with just a tiny nip of autumn in the air. The garden was looking tidy. Norridge felt exceedingly well and had even succeeded in making Yorkshire pudding that morning to go with the beef he was cooking for lunch. Since old Bertie had revealed himself to be such a hopeless cook, Norridge had decided to get interested in cooking. He'd sent the Meals on Wheels ladies packing and bought himself a cookery book called *The Beginner's Guide to Good Cooking*. And he was enjoying inventing meals. He made a lot of mess in the kitchen, of course, but even old Bert had to admit that his cooking was quite good. 'Better than the Social Services' muck!' Norridge said proudly.

At this moment, having pinned up his WELCOME sign, Norridge heard the car come up his lane and he called to the dog, who came bounding to him and sat near him with his ears pricked.

'Here they come!' Norridge said to Garibaldi, and gently scratched the dog's neck. 'It's Bertie-boy and those other nincompoops. Here they are!'